A Thug Made For Me 2
A BBW LOVE STORY

P. WISE

P. WISE PUBLICATIONS
P.O Box 923
Brookhaven, PA 19015

Copyright © 2024 P. Wise
All rights reserved. Published by P. Wise Publications

Including the right to reproduce this book or portions thereof, in any form. No part of this text may be reproduced in any form without the written permission of the author.

This book is a work of fiction. Names, characters, places and incidents are either the product of the author's imagination or are used fictionally. Any resemblance to actual persons, living or dead, or to actual events or locales is entirely coincidental.

www.Prettiwise.com

Credits:

Edited by: 2 Cents Proofreading & Editing

Cover Design: P. Wise (The Wise Company)

Formatting: P. Wise (The Wise Company)

Contents

Stay Connected! 5
Also by P. Wise 7
Synopsis 11
Previously in A Thug Made For Me (Book One) 13

1. Indigo "Indi" Taylor-Anderson 25
2. Quesnel "Quest" MacQuoid 35
3. Indigo 45
4. Khaleef "Kha" Amin 51
5. Quest 63
6. Indigo 73
7. Naim "Nai" Davis 83
8. Indigo 93
9. Quest 101
10. Indigo 111
11. Kha 127
12. Naomi "Nomi" Moore 139
13. Indigo 155
14. Quest 165
15. Indigo 175
16. Quest 183
17. Indigo 195
18. Quest 205

Up Next!	217
Acknowledgments	219
About the Author	221
Stay Connected!	223
Also by P. Wise	225

Stay Connected!

Website/Mailing List: PrettiWise.com
Instagram: @CEO.Pwise / @Authoress.P.Wise

Facebook: Author P. Wise
Facebook Group: Words of the Wise (P. Wise Book Group)
Email: Author.P.Wise@gmail.com

P.O Box 923
Brookhaven, PA 19015

Also by P. Wise

A Thug Made For Me: A BBW Love Story

Summer Nights between Thick Thighs: A Short BBW Erotica

Pretti & The Beast: An Arranged Marriage

Bound to a Savage

Wet Dreams on Lockdown: Lieutenant Grace (Prequel to Bound to a Savage)

Entangled with a Trinidadian Boss

Melted the Heart of a Menace

My Curves Captivated a Hood Millionaire: A BBW Love Story

My Curves Captivated a Hood Millionaire: A BBW Love Story 2

Come Play In It: An Urban Erotica

Heir to the Plug's Throne

Heir to the Plug's Throne 2

Gorgeous Gangstas

Gorgeous Gangstas 2

Gorgeous Gangstas 3

Luchiano Mob Ties: Snatched Up by a Don Spin-Off

Snatched Up by a Don: A BBW Love Story

Snatched Up by a Don: A BBW Love Story 2

Snatched Up by a Don: A BBW Love Story 3

A Saint Luv'n A Savage: A Philly Love Story

Luv'n a Philly Boss: A Saint Luv'n a Savage Spin-off

Kwon: Clone of a Savage

Kwon: Clone of a Savage 2

Summer Luvin' with a NY Baller

Diary of a Brooklyn Girl

Sex, Scams, & Brisks

Sex, Scams, & Brisks 2

Dedication

This book is dedicated to my loyal reader, moderator, and friend:

Denay Lewis

May you rest in peace.

Synopsis

In *A Thug Made For Me 2: A BBW Love Story*, Indigo is finally finding the happiness she craved with Quest, a man who seems to be everything she never knew she needed. However, in typical fashion, just as life starts to smooth out, it throws a curveball. News about her health leaves Indigo teetering between joy and fear, with only Quest to lean on. But as the couple grows closer, Indigo's past resurfaces, threatening to rip them apart.

Quest, meanwhile, finds himself juggling the burdens of his world as he navigates loyalty, love, and the gritty realities of life on the streets. With a trusted ally, Kha, by his side, Quest is forced to make tough decisions, seeking retribution for the losses he's suffered.

The stakes are high, and as one issue resolves, another emerges, pulling Quest deeper into more conflict.

Together, Indigo and Quest must fight not only for their relationship but for their futures, battling both external threats and inner demons.

Will they find a way back to each other, or will their love story be yet another casualty of the harsh world they're entangled in? This urban fiction thriller blends romance and mystery with heart-pounding suspense, keeping you on the edge of your seat 'til the very last page.

Previously in A Thug Made For Me (Book One)

Since the day I threw up, which was about a week beforehand, I'd been out of it. Certain smells had me nauseous, I couldn't keep any food down, and I was feeling as tired as ever. I figured I had gotten food poisoning or something, but it didn't feel like I was getting better, so I decided to go to the doctor was the best choice.

The morning of my scheduled appointment had arrived. When I woke up, Quest had already gone to work. I felt him kiss me on my forehead, as usual, before leaving. Sliding out of the bed slowly so I don't feel too dizzy, I walked to the bathroom to get myself ready. By the time I was finished, I didn't want to go anywhere but back into my bed.

I called Naomi to see if she could have gone with me to my doctor's appointment. When I asked her, she didn't hesitate to come pick me up and go with me. I could've called Quest, but I didn't want to bother him with my problems when he was working to take care of us. Plus, his PO was a pain in the ass, from what I heard. He would randomly pop up to check in on him.

"Do you want me to go inside with you?" Naomi asked as we parked.

"Can you, please?"

She cut the engine. "Let's go."

We both exited the car and made our way inside the doctor's office. It was my first time going to this doctor. Naomi recommended her since I needed someone new and not connected to Malachi.

I filled out the questionnaire form that the nurse gave me. After waiting about half an hour, my name was finally called. I went to the back, where a nurse took my vitals and asked me questions like, what brought me in to see the doctor? I was then asked to give a urine test to check if I was pregnant and then to wait until the doctor called my name. I went and joined Naomi back in the waiting room.

After what seemed to be forever, I was then called to see the doctor.

"I'll be right here, boo," Naomi assured me as I stood up.

I nodded, then took my time walking to the door that led to the doctor's office in the back. At any moment, I felt like I could've fallen out. That's how weak I was.

Once in the doctor's office, she walked in all happy, but once she saw my appearance of discomfort, she took it down a couple of notches.

"Hi, I'm Dr. Bennett. What's going on?" she sympathetically inquired.

"I've been sick, throwing up for the past week. I could hardly keep any food or liquids down," I explained as she read my chart.

"And I see here you mentioned something about hearing loss? How long has that been going on?" She creased her brows together.

I made sure to mention the hearing issue I'd been experiencing to the nurses. If I continued to put it off to get checked out, I wouldn't know what was going on with me.

"Honestly, about a year now."

"And describe it for me." She started to take notes.

"One minute, I can hear fine, and then the next, it becomes muffled, and it sounds like the wind is blowing in my ear."

She nodded. "Okay. I'm going to order some bloodwork for you, along with a hearing test, which you will do now," she informed me.

"Okay, no problem."

"I'll be right back."

Dr. Bennett left out of the room, leaving me sitting there wondering what was really happening to me.

Not long after, a nurse knocked, then walked in with a cart carrying a machine.

"Hi, I'm Nurse Michelle. I'm here to administer the hearing loss test, okay?"

"Okay."

She placed headphones on my ears, then handed me two plastic sticks that had buttons on them. "When you hear a noise in the right ear, press the right button. When you hear it in the left ear, press the left one. Okay?" she directed.

"Yeah, got it."

"Okay, we're about to start now." She fixed back the headphones on my ears.

The beeps started loud in the beginning, but as we went on, it got lower and lower to the point I didn't hear any beeps for a while, so I stopped pressing the buttons. Nurse Michelle would look at me with squinted eyes as if I were supposed to hear something, but I didn't.

After about ten minutes, we concluded the test, and a graph of some sort started printing out some papers. Nurse Michelle gathered them and rested them on top of the machine. She then came and took the equipment off me.

"Dr. Bennett will be back in shortly," she informed me, then exited the room with the cart.

I sat there for another ten minutes alone before the doctor came back into the room. At that time, she had a bunch of papers in her hands.

"Hey, Indigo. So, we've got some things to talk about," she began.

I shifted in my seat. "Like what?" I eyed her.

"From the hearing test, it appears you're experiencing hearing loss. Because of this, we now have to send you to an otolaryngologist for further testing and diagnosis. I'm not an expert in that field, but based on my experience with similar patients, we confirmed it as hearing loss. We just need to figure out how severe it is," she explained.

The news didn't come as a surprise to me because I'd already had it in my head that's what was happening. I could say I was in partial denial. I was praying it wasn't that, but hearing it being my reality struck me in a bad way. Was I going to be completely deaf one day? I asked myself.

"Okay," I spoke lowly. I didn't have much to say on the matter.

"In other news, I did find out why you're so sick," she declared.

"Why?" I raised a brow.

She pulled out a piece of paper and showed it to me. "Congratulations, Ms. Taylor. You're pregnant," Dr. Bennett disclosed.

"What?" I raised my voice in disbelief. "This can't be right."

"Why? You're not happy about this?"

"It's not that. I thought I couldn't get pregnant. I'd been trying for so long with my—"

I didn't want to finish my sentence and sound like a hoe, but I needed to know.

Clearing my throat, I got myself together to speak. "I have been trying for a long time with my husband, and we have never had any success. I just got into a new relationship, and I'm already pregnant. How?" I was so confused.

"It could be two things. One, your husband probably had a vasectomy without your knowledge," she stated.

"But someone else got pregnant by him, so it can't be that," I shot back.

"Or, two, it wasn't in God's plan for you to carry his child."

Those words hit me like a ton of bricks. I never thought about it that way. For some time, I thought something was wrong with me since I couldn't conceive. However, when I went to get checked, all my labs would come back normal.

When God has a plan, he has a plan, and no man could alter it, I thought.

"Hey, cheer up. You're a soon-to-be mom. That's a blessing," she encouraged.

"Thank you." I smiled.

It had been a while since I felt I had a purpose on earth. Getting the news of the baby made me feel alive again.

Although Quest has been helping to revive the old me, the baby inside of me puts the cherry on top of things.

My only worry, though, was Malachi finding out about Quest and the baby before he signed the divorce papers. And I had no other choice but to let Quest know what was going on with my marriage and that we were going to be parents — me for the first time and him again.

God help me.

Naomi dropped me off at home before heading back to work. I told her both the news about my hearing and the baby. She was ecstatic as ever and was already claiming the godmother's title. She said the same thing Dr. Bennett said about the baby being a blessing. Naomi made sure to let me know she was going to be there for me to help with the baby and also with whatever I had to go through with my hearing.

While she was supportive of everything, the main person who needed to be on board didn't know any of what transpired at the doctor's. Since I was feeling a little better, I decided to go and see him. It was killing me inside to hold all these things from Quest — the marriage, the hearing loss, and now the baby. It was a lot.

Before leaving the apartment, I took the meds Dr. Bennett gave me to help with the morning sickness. Trying my luck, I made a sandwich to eat and drank some ginger ale to wash it down and calm my stomach.

Finally heading downstairs, I jumped in my car and made my way to Broad and Olney. On the ride there, I blasted Summer Walker while I sang my lungs out. I was so in tune with the music and practicing to be on American Idol that I didn't notice I was pulling up at the shop.

The gate was closed, so I thought they were out in the field or something. I clicked the call button next to Quest's name in my phone.

"Wassup, Chunks?" he answered on the second ring.

"Hey, bae. I came by the shop, but I see you guys aren't here."

"Are you outside now?" he quizzed.

"Yeah."

"Ard. I'm coming." He hung up.

Moments later, the gate opened, and Quest walked out, looking fine as ever. He jumped in the passenger seat before I could even get out of the car.

He leaned over and pecked my lips. "You cool, mama?" he asked, looking me up and down.

"Yeah, I'm feeling a little better now. Not a hundred percent, but better."

"Good."

"Quesnel, I need to talk to you about some things," I started.

"Ard. Wassup?"

I took a deep breath, then let it out. "I went to the doctor today, and I found out I'm losing my hearing," I revealed.

Quest turned in his seat to face me. "You sure?"

I nodded as tears started to fall. Hearing someone tell me was one thing, but for me to say it out of my own mouth made it so much more real. I started to choke up, and Quest pulling me in for a hug didn't help. I just broke down crying.

"Shhh, shhh, shhh. Everything's gon' be ard, baby," he sympathized. "Don't even trip. We gon' get through this shit." He rubbed my back. We stayed in an embrace for a while without uttering a word.

His phone started to ring, ending the moment. When he looked at who was calling, he groaned in aggravation.

"Hello?" he answered and listened. "Today?" he listened again. "Ard," he told the person, then hung up and looked at me. "That was my PO. I have a random drug test to go and take right now. Can we finish this talk later at home?"

I nodded as I wiped my tears away. "Yeah, we can," I answered. "I can take you to see your PO. I wasn't doing anything after I left here," I offered.

"Ard. Let me go tell Kha I'll be right back." He got out of the car and went into the shop while I waited.

Since I still wasn't all the way feeling better, Quest took the wheel and drove to his PO's office himself while I played passenger princess. The ride wasn't long. We arrived in about ten minutes.

I looked around the building and saw it was state probation he was reporting to. Between the time Quest and I got to know each other and got together, I never asked him if he had done state or federal time. However, it was clear that it was state time when I saw the building sign.

Malachi was a state probation officer. I wasn't sure which office he worked at, but I just knew he spent a lot of his time out in the field rather than behind a desk.

"Come on," Quest told me as he opened his door.

"No, baby, I'm good. Go ahead," I declined.

"He's been wanting to meet you, anyway. You're here. You might as well just pop in with me," he persuaded.

The last thing I wanted, or needed, was for that office to be the same one Malachi worked at or one of his co-workers to recognize me. Or maybe I was just overthinking shit.

"Okay, okay." Against my better judgment, I got out of the car and let him on the sidewalk.

Hand in hand, we entered the building and went

through the security checkpoint. Once through, we made our way to Quest's PO's office. By the time we reached it, the secretary told Quest to go inside, so he knocked and pushed the door open.

When we walked inside, my heart dropped to the pit of my stomach, and I felt like I was about to throw up.

"Indigo?" Malachi quizzed.

Quest looked between the both of us, confused as hell. "How do you know my girl?" he pressed him.

Malachi started to chuckle as he made his way from behind his desk. "Because your girl is my wife."

Oh, fuck!

Indigo TAYLOR

"Indigo, please calm down and breathe," Naomi coached. "Deep breath in and let it out."

I was having a panic attack, something I was used to having when I was overly stressed, and what I had just gone through a little earlier was beyond stressful. Naomi kept talking to me, but her voice became muffled after a while. I would look at her lips here and there, so I knew she was still talking, but I didn't know what she was saying.

Raising my hand, I motioned for her to stop talking. "Please, just give me a minute," I heard myself say in a dull tone.

I sat on the couch at Naomi's place and rested my head back as the entire scene from earlier replayed in my head.

Quest's head snapped in my direction. "What the fuck he mean, wife?" *he scolded.*

"Ques—" I started but was immediately cut off.

"Nigga, you heard me. That's my wife. My bitch." Malachi raised his voice, then turned to me. "You're really fuckin' with a nigga who just came home and ain't got shit?"

"Dickhead, who the fuck you talkin' 'bout like that?" Quest rushed over toward Malachi.

I quickly stepped in between the two of them. "Stop! No!" I shouted.

"Indigo, get out my way!" Quest growled with his eyes trained on Malachi.

Quest looked so hurt and angry. I couldn't take being the reason he was feeling the way he was. And I knew he was even more frustrated because he couldn't react the way he wanted to because of who Malachi was.

"I wish this nigga would. Your goofy ass would be right back behind bars if you even think you can touch me," Malachi taunted.

The door to the office swung open, and two men stood in the doorway. "Is everything alright in here?" one questioned.

Quest turned and looked at them. "Everything's solid." He started to walk toward them to leave.

"Where do you think you're going?" Malachi called out to him.

"Mali, leave him alone, please," I begged.

Malachi went into his drawer and pulled out a clear plastic bag with a urinal cup inside. "You owe me one of these, Mr. MacQuoid." *He wore a smug look.*

Quest turned back around, walked toward Malachi, and snatched the bag out of his hand.

"Administer that for me," *Malachi told one of the guys who was at the door.*

Quest swiftly left out of the office to do the drug test. As I was making my way out to follow him, Malachi rushed and grabbed my arm, quickly closing the door.

"Get off me!" *I grilled as I snatched my arm away from him.*

"This where your ass been? Fuckin' around with a felon? You forgot you're a married woman, Indigo? I should kill you and him." *He stepped closer to me.*

I took a step toward him to show I wasn't intimidated. "I dare you to," *I boldly threatened.*

He looked away and chuckled. "Bitch, I'll show you a whole other side of me you didn't know existed." *He shot me a menacing glare that sent chills throughout my body.*

I'd never seen Malachi that way before. Although there were times he would talk recklessly, he never threatened me or gave off any vibe that he would hurt me.

I swallowed the lump that formed in my throat. "Why are you doing this? You don't want me, so just leave me alone," *I pleaded.*

He tilted his head. "What makes you think I'll allow you to skip into the fuckin' sunset with another man? A man like him, anyway? Over my dead body, Indigo. Wrap that shit up and bring yo' ass home."

I stepped back some. "And if I don't?" I challenged.

"Be home tonight, or else," he gave me an ultimatum.

I quickly turned and rushed out of his office. As I looked for Quest, I saw the man who took him to do his drug test.

"Hi, where did he go?" I questioned.

The man looked past me, which made me turn around. Malachi was in his doorway, staring at us.

"He left, ma'am," he informed me.

"Thank you." I rolled my eyes and walked off, leaving out of the building.

When I reached outside, there was no sight of Quest. I called his phone multiple times, but he kept declining my call. That's when I knew he was more upset than I thought.

I got into my car, and before I could start it up, a river of tears started to flow from my eyes. My body shook as my breathing picked up. How could you let this shit happen? I asked myself.

There was no doubt in my mind that I fucked up badly. It was no one else to blame but myself for everything that was happening. Maybe I should've just told Quest everything from the moment we met. Maybe I should've kept things platonic and not get romantically involved. Or maybe I should've just stayed with Malachi. All sorts of thoughts plagued my mind. I couldn't think straight.

"Indigo, Indigo," Naomi called out to me loudly, bringing me back into the present with her.

"Yeah?" I answered.

"Did you hear anything I said?" she quizzed.

"Honestly, I didn't. I'm sorry." I covered my face with both of my hands.

As she was about to speak, someone began knocking on her door. "Give me a second." She rose from her seat across from me and went to see who it was.

I laid back on the couch and stared at the ceiling. My mind was discombobulated, and I couldn't focus properly. There was only one person on my mind — Quesnel MacQuoid.

"What are you doing here?" I heard Naomi ask someone.

"What you mean, what I'm doing here? When the fuck did I need to have a reason?" a man spoke.

"I didn't mean it that way, bae. My friend is here, and she's going through something serious right now, and she needs me."

"A friend, huh?"

"Indi, say hi," she instructed me.

"Hi," I spoke loud enough for him to hear it was a female. *Insecure ass niggas*, I thought.

The way Naomi's apartment was set up, her living room wasn't visible from the front door, so he couldn't see inside.

"Oh, ard. Go ahead, then. Hit me when she leaves," he told her.

Moments later, the door was closed, and Naomi made her way back inside to the living room.

"Girl, I can leave. I don't want to be in the way," I offered.

She sucked her teeth and waved her hands. "Chile, please. That nigga will be fine." We both started laughing.

"Is that your man or boo thang?" I pried.

I sincerely wanted to know what my friend had going on. For the past few months, I felt it was all about me and Quest. I surely didn't want to come off as a selfish and self-centered friend.

"He's my boo thing that's slowly turning into something serious. What I can say is he's the only nigga I'm fuckin' with right now and giving up this coochie too."

"Okay then. Well, I hope it works out for you, baby."

"Yeah, me too." She smiled. "Anyway, back to you. What are you going to do?"

The faint smile I had quickly went away. "I don't know. What should I do?"

"I can't tell you what to do. I could only suggest something, and then it'll be up to you whether you want to do it or not."

"I just want my man," I pleaded.

"We're talking about Quest, right?"

I shot her a devilish glare. "You shouldn't even have to ask."

She raised her hands in surrender. "Hey, I was just making sure," she retorted. "If you want your man, then go get him. Sit him down and explain everything, leaving not one detail out."

I sighed out loud. "What if Quest doesn't even want to hear me out?" Tears welled in my eyes at the thought.

"He will hear you out, boo. Just make it known to him you want him and not that nut-ass husband of yours. Plus, you have his seed growing inside of you. Did you tell him yet?"

"No, I haven't had the chance to tell him much of anything, for real, for real."

"Well, use that as your way in to soften him up. If he's a real nigga, once he hears about the baby, he'll melt."

"Yeah, you're right," I agreed.

We talked some more about the situation and possible outcomes. After feeling completely drained, she offered for me to stay the night just to let things die down. I went to bed, missing the fuck out of Quest and hating Malachi even more than I already did.

THE FOLLOWING DAY, I WOKE UP LOOKING around Naomi's living room, confused. I forgot where I was and why I was there for a split second. Then, finally, everything rushed back to me about what happened the day before. I had escaped my reality for a few hours, and I would've done anything to escape for a little longer.

The first thing I did was check my phone to see if I had any missed calls or text messages from Quest, but I didn't. But, of course, there were messages from Malachi.

> Malachi: Damn, you got niggas serving me divorce papers at work?

> Malachi: Yeah, you gon' see who's gon' have the last laugh. See you in court, wife.

I rolled my eyes so hard that I felt them in the back of my head. Malachi was the devil himself. I couldn't for the life of me understand why he just didn't let me be. He had his own situation going on. Yet he wanted to have his cake and eat it, too.

After I read his messages, I saw Naomi left me one.

> Naomi: Good morning, boo. I left for work quietly. I didn't want to wake you. You can leave whenever you like. The door has a slam lock on it. If you want to stay longer, mi casa su casa. There are breakfast things to cook, along with a bunch of other food. Help yourself. Love you! And don't be over there crying, either.

I giggled at her humor. If it was one thing Naomi was going to do, it was lighten up the mood when she needed to.

After looking at the time on my phone, which read *nine twenty-three* a.m., I went into the bathroom to freshen up. I barely had an appetite, so I didn't bother to raid her kitchen. The nausea was coming on, so I didn't want to eat anything and bring it back up.

Within half an hour, I was walking out of her door and heading to my car. The walk had me feeling weak, so I quickly shuffled my feet to get into the car before I fell out. I was only a month into my pregnancy, and I was experiencing hell.

Safely behind the wheel, I started up the car, took a deep breath, and drove off. I was happy Naomi didn't live too far from me, so the drive wasn't long. In less than fifteen minutes, I was pulling up home and parking.

I slowly made my way upstairs to the apartment.

Walking off the elevator, I felt relief once I saw the door. I was dying to get inside to get my medication to help me feel better so that I could finally eat something. I pushed the key into the hole and turned it. When I walked in, the place felt still, which I expected. Around that time, Quest would've usually been at work, so I knew I had time to whine down and get myself together before he came back home.

Kicking off my UGG slides, I made my way down the hall toward our bedroom. As I was passing the guest bathroom, heading for the door, I turned and was facing the barrel of a gun.

QUESNEL
Quest
MACQUOID

"Fuck, I almost blew your fuckin' brains out," I scoffed, lowering my Glock.

I heard someone come into the apartment, and with everything that went down, I wasn't sure who the fuck it was walking in.

Before walking off, I shot Indigo a look of disappointment. She betrayed me, just like everyone else did. I poured my heart out to that woman, told her my scars, my secrets, and she stood there and played me like a fool. She wore a mask because I had no idea who the fuck she really was.

When I glanced back, I saw that Indigo was still stuck in the same spot. She looked shocked and unable to move. Any other time I would've cared, but then and there, I didn't give two fucks about how she felt.

"You're seriously going to pull a gun on me, Quest?" Indigo questioned with a surprised look.

I turned around with the quickness. "You playin' right?" I curled my upper lip.

"Quest..."

"Don't fuckin' call my name. I don't trust a soul right now, and death could've been walkin' through that door. So, I pulled my gun first. Fuck questions."

"Who would be coming here besides me?"

"What the fuck you mean? It could've been anybody walking in this apartment. You could've given the keys to ol' boy. Seeing as though yo' ass ain't come home last night, you must've gone back to your husband," I snapped, then started to chuckle. "A fuckin' husband," I whispered in disbelief.

"Quest, it's not what you think. I—"

"Indigo, you're married. It's no way around that shit. When you meet someone and start to get involved, that's something you should mention. Damn!"

"I know, I was—"

Bang. Bang. Bang.

Both of our heads snapped in the direction of the front door. I walked past her and eased my way to the door with my gun drawn. Indigo followed close behind.

Bang. Bang. Bang.

"Quesnel MacQuoid. It's Philly police. Open up!" a man shouted from the other side.

My heart immediately sank as paranoia kicked in. *What the fuck are they here for?* I asked myself. I quickly hid my Glock in the secret compartment I had in my room's closet. I knew if I was to get caught with it, I was definitely doing another ten because I already had felonies to my name.

"Open the door, Indi," I instructed as I walked out of the closet.

"You sure?" she asked with her hands on the doorknob.

I walked down the corridor toward her. "Go ahead."

She hesitated for a moment but then unlocked and opened the door.

Four African American police officers rushed in toward me. Before they could reach me, I raised my hands in the air in surrender. I wanted to show them I wasn't resisting arrest, although I had no idea what I was being arrested for.

The whole situation felt like déjà vu. My nightmare came flashing before me as they tackled me to the ground and started punching and kicking on me. The only difference was that I wasn't being shot, and I didn't feel the heat coming from the fire, but I still heard their cries in the distance.

"What are you doing? He isn't resisting!" I heard Indigo scream.

Catching a blow to my lip, I immediately tasted blood and was ready to kill something. However, I knew I would've been in deeper shit if I had only fought back, so I curled up as much as I could during the attack.

"Stop! Stop!" Indigo continued to yell.

"Shut the fuck up!" one officer told her.

"Make me," she hissed back.

"I won't have to. I'll let your husband handle that."

At that moment, that's when everything made sense to me. Anderson's bitch ass sent them after me.

"Fuck you!" she spewed.

"Yeah, yeah. You're just salty your little boyfriend finna get put away." He snicked. "Get him up."

As a team, they all picked up my heavy body, making me stand on my feet.

"You've violated probation, bull. We gotta take your nut-ass in," the same officer ridiculed.

How the fuck is this even possible?

Instead of hanging my head in defeat, I lifted that shit up high and walked out of the apartment, then the building altogether. Once I was placed in the back of a squad SUV, I closed my eyes and said a silent prayer. I needed God to not only get me out of the situation I was in but to give me patience and tolerance.

The entire ride to wherever they were taking me, I thought about how stupid I was for falling for Indigo. Without a doubt, I felt my blurred judgment had something to do with not being intimate with a woman for such a long period of time. It's like I got the pussy and got stupid, which wasn't my character at all.

I really thought Indigo was it for me. The way shorty made me feel was out of this world. She knew how to treat a nigga, take care of a nigga, and be there for a nigga, but apparently, it was all a game for her.

The way karma worked, I never wanted to be on her bad side when it came to messing with married women. I would fuck on a bitch that had a nigga, but not one who was in a union bound by God or the law. That was the kind of shit I couldn't get down with because I wouldn't want anyone fucking on the woman I gave my last name to. I just couldn't properly wrap my head around that shit. It had me fucked up. My emotions were all over the place. I didn't know how to feel, and I honestly didn't want to feel.

When we finally arrived at our destination, I looked out and saw we were at PICC (Philadelphia Industrial Correctional Center). They skipped the whole precinct and took me straight to prison. After I was processed, I was informed I would go to court first thing in the morning to go before the judge.

Instead of taking me into a unit, I was placed in a holding cell for the night, where I was uncomfortable like shit. My mind was so busy with different shit on it that I couldn't even sleep. All I wanted to do was see the judge to know my fate.

THE FOLLOWING MORNING, I WAS WIDE AWAKE and ready for them to transport me to court. With no sleep and a ton of weight on my shoulders, I was exhausted as hell. I was shackled, then placed on the bus with another niggas to head to court. Before I knew it, we were pulling up to the courthouse and being unloaded into holding cells.

While everyone else was trying to find reasons to talk to one another, I kept my mind focused on what was about to happen. It was my first time being in that predicament, but I'd heard so many fucked up stories about judges giving harsh punishments for violators depending on the violation. The thing was, I didn't even know what the fuck I did to violate besides fuckin' on that man's wife.

After sitting for about an hour and a half, I was finally

called on to go see the judge. They didn't allow me to get any phone calls, so I couldn't even call Kha to let him know anything or to get me a lawyer. Walking to the courtroom, I prayed the public defender I got was solid enough to fight for me, although they didn't know me.

The moment I walked in, my eyes landed on Indigo, but I quickly shifted my gaze. I then saw Kha sitting close to her and Anderson's goofy ass behind the prosecutor's table. The Marshal escorted me to the table next to an African American man who looked like he was young, around his early thirties, and green as hell.

"Hi, I'm Thomas. I'll be representing you today," the nerd greeted me as I took my seat.

"What they got on me?" I asked, cutting right to the chase.

"It looks like you pissed dirty," he revealed.

I dropped my head and shook it. "How? I don't even smoke. I don't do drugs and barely drink," I expressed.

He shrugged his shoulders with a confused face. "It's right here." He showed me the report from the test. "They have you red-handed. The best thing to do is take accountability and be remorseful for your actions."

"Nigga!" I raised my voice, making everyone look my way. "Didn't you hear me? I don't smoke," I whispered in a harsh tone.

"Is everything alright, counselor?" the judge asked.

Thomas looked up and nodded. "Everything is fine, thanks," he responded. "This will be hard to prove that you didn't piss dirty when it's right here, Mr. MacQuoid."

The way he kept giving me pushback about standing up for me, I knew it was over. I was definitely going under, and it wasn't shit I could do about it.

While the judge, the prosecutor, and my weak ass lawyer went back and forth, I was zoned out in another world. I couldn't say shit or do anything, so it was pointless for me to even pay attention. When the judge was about to sentence me, that's when I came back to reality.

"The defendant will serve six months in..." the judge started.

After I heard the amount of time I had, everything else became a blur for me. While six months wasn't shit to me after I did a whole decade, it was fucked up because I was being punished for falling for the wrong fuckin' woman — another man's wife.

With nothing else to say to the lawyer, I stood to my feet and had the Marshal escort me out. While walking, I glimpsed over to see Anderson sitting down, wearing a devilish grin on his face... one that read, I won. Indigo had tears in her eyes, but the shit didn't move me, not one bit.

Kha shot me a head nod. I lifted my hands to my ears, gesturing that I'd call him. Indigo must have informed him of me getting snatched up. I appreciated the fact he showed up. Every day, Khaleef had been proving his worth, his loyalty, and his support to me. He was truly the clone of his father. It looked like he was all I had, and I told myself I would've had to be okay with that.

Indigo TAYLOR

As I sat there watching them take Quest away, all I could feel was guilt and misery. If I could've, I would've jumped up, saved him, and rescued him from the fucked-up system. I saw firsthand how people who were put in a position to protect civilians from criminals abused their power. Malachi showed me another side to him, and there was no turning back. I wanted nothing to do with him.

Once Quest left out of the courtroom, I finally mustered up enough energy to get up to leave. As I was walking out, Malachi approached me with a snug look.

"I told you I was gon' see you in court." He smirked, referring to the encrypted text message he wrote me when

I was at Naomi's spot. I thought he was talking about divorce court. The whole time, he already had shit brewing.

Without uttering a word to him, I rushed off and exited through the courtroom doors. The hallway was busy with all kinds of people dealing with legal matters. I maneuvered my way through conversations of different cases, as my main focus was to get out of the building. What started as loud voices around me quickly turned into muffles, and before I knew it, I heard nothing but wind.

My body started to feel weaker than usual because I hadn't eaten anything. With no food in my system and my emotions all over the place, I was bound to fall out.

Knowing that Quest was locked up because of me made me sick to my stomach. He didn't acknowledge me or want to look my way. I could only imagine what was going through his head. One thing was for sure: he blamed me for everything that was happening to him.

Once I reached the outside of the building, I took a deep breath in and let it out.

"Indigo," I heard someone call my name.

When I turned, I saw Quest's friend, Khaleef, walking up to me.

"Oh, hi," I greeted him with a faint smile.

I wasn't sure what Quest had told him or how much he knew about the whole situation, so I was feeling kind of embarrassed. When the police first came to the apartment to arrest him, I went over to the tire shop and informed Kha. Judging by his appearance for court, he did his due diligence and found out he had court that morning.

"You cool?" he inquired in a sincere tone.

I nodded. "I'll be fine."

"Where you parked?"

I pointed toward the garage. "The garage on Sansom."

"Ard. Me too. Come on." He motioned for me to follow him.

The weather was nice that day, so we walked at a decent pace down the block to the parking garage.

"Six months ain't shit to him, but we gotta get him out of there," he exclaimed.

"I agree. This shit is so unfair. There's something we can do, right?"

"Not us personally, but a good lawyer, yeah. We gotta get them to appeal the judge's sentence and the violation altogether," he recommended.

"Do you know anyone?"

"Yeah, I do. When I talk to Quest, I'll see what he wants me to do."

"Okay. Just let me know how I could help," I offered.

The least I could do was do any and everything in my power to help undo the situation. There was no taking back what Malachi did, but at least the system could see that there was a personal vendetta behind the violation.

"I'll keep you posted."

We finally reached the garage, and he walked me to my car first. As we were approaching it, I felt a little lightheaded, and before I knew it, I was throwing up right there on the ground.

"Oh shit," Kha blurted out.

I was trying to gather myself after bringing up nothing but fluids since I had nothing solid on my stomach.

"You ard?" Kha inquired.

I lifted my finger, letting him know to give me a moment.

"Damn, you pregnant or something?" he wondered.

My eyes bucked as I slowly looked over at him. He shot me back a surprised look.

"Shit, you are pregnant," he raised his voice.

Before I could properly respond, Kha's eyes shifted somewhere with a confused look, which made me turn around.

"You pregnant?" Malachi questioned with disgust on his face.

Immediately, Kha stepped up in between us. "Ain't none of that bullshit going on here," he told Malachi.

"Mind your fuckin' business. This is between me and my wife."

"Clearly, she doesn't want shit to do with you. And from my knowledge, this is my boy woman."

Malachi took a step closer to him. "Bull, move."

Kha stepped up again, bringing them face-to-face. "I ain't your parolee, nigga. I'll fuck you up without thinking twice, goofy ass nigga."

Malachi started laughing and backed away. "I'll see you, Indi. In the meantime, make sure my baby's good."

"This ain't your baby, fool," I finally spoke up.

He laughed as he walked off. More and more, I saw a deranged side to Malachi. He should've known the baby wasn't his. I was with him for years, and I didn't get pregnant. As soon as I left him and opened my legs for someone else, I received a blessing. God had a crazy way of setting things up, but who was I to question him?

Once Malachi was gone, Kha turned to me. "Does Quest know?" He raised a brow.

"No. I was trying to tell him, but everything just happened so quickly," I explained.

He nodded. "It's gon' be ard. Come on, get in the car." Kha walked me over and opened the door. "Are you good to drive?"

I nodded. "Yeah, I'm good. Thanks a lot for that."

"Ain't nuffin', man. I'm just doing what my nigga would've wanted me to do. Take my number and hit me when you get home."

We exchanged numbers, then I started up my car and pulled out of the parking spot. As I made my way out of the garage and onto the bustling streets of Philadelphia, my mind went straight to Quest. I needed to talk to him to see where his head was at. But most of all, I needed to know I still had his heart and if we were going to be okay.

KHALEEF "KHA" AMIN JR.

I couldn't believe the nut shit my boy was going through. Although Indigo was the reason her goofy ass husband violated Quest, it still wasn't her direct fault. Most people would say it was all on her, but I saw it differently. That girl loved the fuck out of Quest, and her old nigga couldn't handle being replaced.

The public defender this nigga had was a straight-up ass. I mean, he didn't even try to fight for my nigga. When Indigo came by the shop to tell me what happened, I got on the line with my pops' lawyer, but he was out of town handling a federal case. He said he would've been back in a few days, but Quest's court date had already gone. I made a mental note to call him when he got back after briefly speaking to Indigo about getting Quest to appeal his case.

By the time I reached home from going to court for Quest, I received a text from Indigo letting me know she made it home safely. It was one thing for her to be stressed out about the situation, but to be pregnant and stressed was an entirely different thing. I was a cold-hearted muthafucker who didn't care about much, only family and those in my circle, but my heart went out to Indigo.

THE NEXT MORNING, I WOKE UP FEELING optimistic. It was the day of my family court case hearing. My sixteen-year-old daughter's mother put me up for child support and was trying to get retro payments from since she was born. The whole shit was just ridiculous and wild. I prayed the judge saw right through her, but I already knew it would be a process.

I rolled out of bed and went to the bathroom to get myself situated. Once I was finished showering and brushing my teeth, I got dressed in the calm black Celine slacks and white button-down shirt. I slid my feet into a pair of shiny black Pradas, then placed my Kufi on my head, covering my freshly cut fade. I looked like a totally different person than I did on a daily basis when dealing with work shit at the tire shop.

As soon as I was dressed, I shot my lawyer a text, letting her know I was on my way to the courthouse. I locked up my place and made my way to my Ranger Rover. I lived in Olney, so it took me about twenty minutes to get to the Philadelphia Family Court on Arch Street.

I found a parking spot, hopped out, and made my way inside of the courthouse.

The moment I spotted the courtroom where my case would be called in, I peeped my lawyer on the phone. She waved me over with a bright smile, so I walked over to her.

She hung the phone up. "Good morning, Khaleef. You clean up well." She sized me up and down.

Ms. Lewis was a young family lawyer who came highly recommended by my pops' criminal lawyer, Cohen. From my research, she was a beast in the courtroom. When I first met her, I thought she was just another pretty face, uppity bitch, but I was wrong. She was well educated and knew her shit.

"Thank you, thank you." I smirked.

"Anyway, today won't be anything long and drawn out. It's only the first date. The judge would want to hear from both sides what they want to happen, and then he'll set another date to have evidence presented," she explained.

"Ard, that's cool."

Just when we were about to make our way inside the courtroom, I saw my daughter's mother, Tatianna, and my beautiful princess, Khadijah.

"Ol' head!" Khadijah shouted when she saw me.

Leaving her mother's side, she lightly jogged over and wrapped her arms around me tight.

"What I told you 'bout callin' me that shit?" I playfully squeezed and shook her.

"You need to stop being in denial. You're old, and it's okay," she shot back.

I didn't understand why she saw me as old because I was only thirty-three years old. Tatianna and I had her when we were only seventeen.

"Yeah, ard." I kissed her on her forehead. "You cool?" I looked down at her.

She pulled away and looked up at me. "No cap, I miss you."

Khadijah was my whole life. She was the reason I grind the way I did and wanted a better life. Baby girl was the most beautiful human being, inside and out. I wasn't sure how she came out to be such a sweetheart with two parents, like myself and her mother. Her mother was once sweet, but then she turned into a bitch after I stopped falling for her games. We could've been one big happy family, but Tatianna was too caught up in her own happiness, and everything had to be her way.

"I miss you too, young. We gon' get shit straightened out, don't even trip."

"Khadijah, let's go," Tatianna snapped.

Dij, what I called her for short, shot me a look, then sauntered off. I felt anger inside me building up, but I had to quickly remember where I was and what I was there for. Tatianna would've tried to use any little thing I did or said against me in court.

"Don't even pay it any mind," Ms. Lewis advised. "Come, let's go inside." She led the way inside the courtroom.

By the time we walked in, our case was being called. As we sat down in our seats, I said a silent prayer. I needed things to work out in my favor.

"Not bad, not bad," I told Ms. Lewis. "Thank you, and keep me posted on everything," I informed her.

The hearing went well on the first day. Just like Ms. Lewis mentioned, it was short and simple. After the judge asked both sides what they wanted, Tatianna wanted child support and back pay on top of it. All I requested was I have shared custody of Khadijah since the mother was keeping her away from me and to not put me on child support since I handle my fatherly duties.

Ms. Lewis went fighting out from out the gate. The judge ordered the attorneys to bring forward all evidence at the next hearing. He also gave an order for Khadijah to be with me from Friday to Sunday. It was a tremendous step in the right direction for me.

"Will do. Call me if you need me." She smiled before walking off, making sure to switch hard. After already getting good results from the case, I was ready to dick her ass down as a reward, especially if she kept looking at me the way she did.

"Dad," I heard Dij's voice, grabbing my attention away from the sexy-ass lawyer to her.

"Yo." I turned around to see her and her mother standing there.

"Can I get some money to go shopping?" she poked her bottom lip out.

I pulled out my wallet and handed her a hundred-dollar bill. "You coming home in two days. We'll go shopping then." I eyed Tatianna.

Dij glimpsed at her mother, then back at me quickly. I didn't trust Tatianna's scamming ass at all. For all I knew, she put Dij up to it to ask me for money.

"Thanks, ol' head." She smiled. "See you Friday." We hugged each other.

I watched them walk away and out of the building before heading out myself. It felt great to know I was about to have my baby girl back in my space after years of bullshit with her mother.

Allah never sleeps, I thought to myself.

A FEW DAYS HAD PASSED, AND FRIDAY QUICKLY arrived. I woke up at the crack of dawn to get ready to make a drive to Dallas, Pennsylvania, to State Correctional Institution Dallas to see my old man. It was something I did at least twice a month in person, while the other times, we would video visit.

The ride was two and a half hours, and thankfully, there was usually no traffic going up to see him since everyone was driving in the opposite direction to go to work in the city. With my music blasting and cruise control on, I got to the facility in no time.

When I parked in the parking lot, I sat back in my seat and just looked at the entrance, then looked around the fencing and wires. It was the one thing that stood in between my father and I. Thinking about the separation had me irate all over again. Before I got deep into my mind and got fully upset, I snapped out of it and prepared myself to go inside. I had to make sure I was back in Philly by the time Dij got out of school at two-thirty. It was my first time having her back after a few years, and I didn't want to be late or break the court order.

Walking into the building, the officers greeted me as usual. They were so used to me coming to visit him that most of them knew who I was. After going through the security process, the staff allowed me to go onto the visiting floor. I waited about ten minutes before I saw him walking out of the back door with a few other inmates. He smiled and bobbed his head up and down as if he were listening to music.

I stood to my feet once he got near me. "Old man," I greeted as we embraced each other.

"Asalaam Walaikum," he greeted.

"Walaikum Asalaam," I answered back.

We were Muslims, so it was how we greeted one another or any other Muslims who came across our path.

"How you ol' head?" I asked as we took our seats.

He shot me a grin. "I'm good, young. I can't

complain," he retorted. "What's the word? How are you?" He eyed me closely.

"I'm good, for the most part. Alhamdulillah," I praised and thanked God.

"Alhamdulillah. How was court the other day?"

"It went well. I got Dij back for the time being. The judge gave me the weekends starting today. So, when I leave from here, I'ma go get ready for her," I excitedly revealed.

"Mashallah!" he exclaimed with joy.

My father loved his granddaughter so much as if she were his own. It pains him that he hadn't been able to see her for some years since his incarceration. Also, her mother wouldn't allow her to talk to him through email, phone, or regular mail.

"Yeah, man. I'm happy as hell. She seems like she is, too."

"Good, good. Whatever you do, make sure you do right by her and don't fuck shit up. Do as the judge says and show them you're fit to be her guardian. She only has two more years before she's eighteen, and then it's a wrap with the system."

"I know, I know. Don't even worry, pops," I assured him.

"Khaleef, I'm serious. Don't make what I did go in vain." He looked at me with a serious expression.

A few years back, I did some wild shit that could've sent me to prison for life. Instead, my father took the wrap for it. It didn't sit right with me, but he made it where I didn't have a choice in his decision. He felt he raised me right, and it was then my turn to do the same for my daughter, but I couldn't have done that behind a prison wall or fence.

My father was my hero since I was a young'n. He was a straight hustler and someone everyone in the hood respected. He loved my mother the way a man should love his wife. He did what he needed to do to take care of his family without any complaints. My pops was the perfect role model, and even while on the inside, he still had a huge impact on my life. That's one of the main reasons I listened to everything he told me to do and trusted his advice.

"You got my word. I won't fuck shit up."

"My boy." He leaned back and smiled. "How's things with Quest?"

He didn't know about the probation violation and the situation with Indigo's husband, so I got him up to speed on everything. Once I was finished, he was in disbelief at the drama but quickly started to think about a resolution.

After we discussed a few more things further, we wrapped up our visit and said our goodbyes for the time being. Watching him walk back through the doors that separated us never got easier. It still felt like the first time I saw him walking through it.

Shaking that fucked up feeling, I shifted my mind to something positive — my baby girl was coming to chill with her daddy for the weekend.

QUESNEL *Quest* MACQUOID

After a few days, I was finally out of the holding cells and onto a unit with the general population at PICC. The cell I got was with a junkie, but it didn't matter to me. As long as he stayed in his place and didn't do any drugs around me, we would be all good.

When I got settled in my cell, I went back into the dayroom to make a phone call. The first person and only person I needed to holla at was Kha. The crazy part was I knew his phone number off the top of my head from when I was getting ready to be released. His pops made me memorize it as if my life depended on it. It worked out in my favor, though.

Walking up to the phones, I saw a group of niggas

around my age and a little younger looking at me. It was the typical prison or jail routine. Niggas wanted to see who they could try to get over on. I was the wrong person for them to try their luck. If they knew better, they'd find something or someone else safer to play with.

I dialed Kha's number, praying he wasn't busy. On the third ring, I heard him answer. The automated system went through the prompts for him to accept.

"Yo, bro," he answered.

"What's good?"

"You tell me, nigga. You good?"

"Yeah, I'm straight. I just can't believe I'm back in this fuckin' place."

"Don't worry, we gon' see what we can do to get you out. Pops told me to have his lawyer take your case and appeal it. You cool with that?" he questioned.

"Nigga, fuck yeah. Get me out of here. Have him come see me ASAP yesterday."

"Say no more."

"When he comes, I'll give him instructions to give you. I don't trust this line or any of these muthafuckers. The phone is always off the hook," I told him, referring to people always listening.

"I got it."

"Ard. I'll give you a call tomorrow. Stay low and handle the business."

"You know what type time we on, ye mean?"

"Mmm-hmm. I'll holla." I hung up.

When I turned to walk away from the phone, the group of niggas were gone. As I walked to my cell, I saw two of them standing outside of it. In my head, I already knew some shit was about to pop off, or at least they were going to try some shit.

I saw another two of them in my room the moment I stepped into the doorway of my cell. That's when I knew my predictions were correct.

"Fuck is this? I know y'all?" I asked the two that were inside my cell, then turned and looked at the two behind me.

"You don't, but you gon' get to know us," one answered.

I chuckled, then flicked my nose with my thumb. "Listen, I don't want no problems. Let me be, and I let y'all be."

They all started laughing. "That ain't how it works, bull. Your name's MacQuoid, though, right?" one asked.

"Who's asking?" I raised a brow.

"A friend of mine, Anderson, paid a nice chunk of bread for us to have a talk with you." He grinned.

"A talk, huh?"

"Yeah, a talk. But if you pay double what he paid, then we're good. No conversation needed. What you think?"

I lowered my head a little and tilted it as if I were thinking. "I think you the bid, and you should get the fuck out of my shit," I retorted, insulting them.

Before I knew it, the two behind me rushed toward me, pushing me into the cell where all four of them jumped on me at once. Each one of them was not any match for my size, so they had to pounce on me together.

As I curled up, I peeped one of them kept kicking me with the same rhythm. So, after timing his kicks, I grabbed onto his foot and pulled him to the ground. On his way down, he knocked over one of the guys next to him. This caused everyone to slow down with the punches and kicks.

Taking the moment in as an advantage, I grabbed the one on the ground and started to deliver blows to his face, breaking his nose on the first hit. Blood immediately spewed all over, making the other three jump on me harder. Once they saw I was fighting back no matter what, one of the guys came behind me and wrapped his arm around my throat while the other one pulled a shank out from his side.

Seeing as though I was being held and in a vulnerable position, a little fear crept in. I wasn't sure if that was it for me or if it was another way out. I quickly thought, did I have a reason to fight? And I remembered I had nothing to fight for. No kid, no woman, no family. Absolutely nothing.

Still, something in me allowed myself to muster up just enough energy to flip the dude over my back at the same time the nigga with the shank was rushing toward me. Instead of the shank stabbing me, it stabbed his own boy. Once he saw the move I made, he became more enraged and started to swing the shank wildly. I ducked and weaved as much as I could, but he slashed my arm one good time.

The alarm went off, and I heard the officers rushing into the unit. Two of the guys ran out of my cell but were tackled by some COs, while the one bled out on my cell floor. I sat on the ground with my back against the wall, holding onto my bloody arm. When the officers rushed my cell, they knocked me upside my head with their batons and sprayed pepper spray.

There was no reason for them to do that when we weren't fighting at that moment or resisting them. Nonetheless, leave it up to COs or any law enforcement that whenever they got an opportunity to fuck up a nigga, they would.

"He just got here," I heard one CO say.

Yeah, and niggas already on my dick, I thought as I felt them try to drag my heavy body out of the unit. I had to get out of that place, one way or another.

THE NEXT MORNING, I WOKE UP, AND I WAS STILL in medical. I winced in pain as I moved my arm, trying to turn on my side. Looking around, I saw I was the only inmate in the room. I figured they sent ol' boy out to the hospital after he got stabbed. Imagine that a person goes to hurt someone with his crew and ends up being the one hurt by the hands of his own people. That's a lesson for Anderson. Don't send weak ass niggas to do his dirty work.

Once my mind wasn't cloudy as before, I was able to process what the fuck happened. Indigo's husband really put money on my head. He wanted me fucked up or gone, and it was no telling the extent he would go.

"MacQuoid, you have a visitor," a CO walked into the room and informed me.

"I ain't even do no visitors' list yet." I was confused.

"It's a legal visit," he clarified.

That makes sense, I thought.

"Oh, ard."

I rose from the bed, swung my legs around, and slipped my feet into the bullshit prison shoes. Once on my feet, I followed the guard out of the room and through the medical department. We made our way through the prison and finally to visitation.

When we walked into the visiting room, he led me to one of the private rooms. Walking in, I saw a Jewish man sitting down, going through some papers. Once he saw I had arrived, he jumped to his feet and extended his hand for me to shake. The guard left us alone.

"Conner Cohen. Nice to meet you," he introduced himself.

"Likewise, I'm Quest." I kept it short and sat down.

"After looking at your case and hearing what happened from Khaleef, I know for a fact we will win," he started.

"I don't need no false hope. Just tell me what it is raw, no sugar coating."

"And I am. It's a win. I just need to gather some evidence to present in the appeal, file it, and wait for them to grant it," he nonchalantly explained.

"That simple?" I raised a brow.

"That simple."

I nodded. "Ard then. What do you need from me?"

"Tell me everything from the start."

I got comfortable in my seat and started to give him the rundown of how Indigo and I met, everything in between until the police came and arrested me. I left the part about the incident inside my cell. I wasn't a snitch. And although I was putting someone on the chopping block to get out, it was the truth I was telling, and Anderson was no street nigga. He was the law.

"Okay, I have everything. I will need to speak with Indigo for a statement, as well as get a few other things from her. Like pictures and documents that you both live together, just proof that you two have a romantic relationship. Also, I'll need her marriage certificate that proves she's legally married to what is now your former probation officer," he explained as he gathered his things.

"Call her. She'll give you whatever you need," I confidently stated, but deep down inside, I wasn't sure what type of time Indigo was on.

"Good." He looked at my arm. "What happened?" he pried.

I looked at it, too, and saw blood was showing. The dressing needed to be changed.

"Nothing I can't handle," I assured him.

"Alright, then. That's it for now. Anything else you need me to do?"

That's when I remembered I had to send a message to Kha with him.

"Yeah, can I get a pen and paper to write something down?"

He gave me what I asked for, and I quickly wrote where to find my stash so Kha could go and get it. The lawyer needed to be paid, and I needed money on my books. Once done, I slid the paper to him.

"Get that to Kha for me," I instructed.

He stood to his feet. "No problem. I will come and see you soon. Here's my card. Call me if you need me and for anything."

"Thank you, Cohen."

We shook hands, and he left out of the room. Moments later, the same guard came and got me to take me back to medical. On my way back, my mind just drifted off, thinking about how shit would've been if I hadn't met Indigo.

Indigo TAYLOR

I was finally walking through my apartment door after a long day of work. For some reason, that day, they had me running around the building more than usual. I was a receptionist. I was supposed to be sitting behind a desk all day. The baby was kicking my ass, as usual, too.

Kicking off my shoes, I went and plopped down on the living room couch, took a deep breath in, and let it out.

"Whew!" I exclaimed out loud.

Knock. Knock.

"Fuck my life," I pleaded.

I had literally just sat down and had to get back up to answer the door. It was Naomi. She told me she was coming over, but I didn't think it would've been when I just rested my ass on the couch.

Walking to the door, the knocks began again.

"I'm coming, damn!" I shouted for her to hear.

When I opened the door, I saw her back turned, and she was talking to someone.

"But who are you here for? Because he ain't here," she mouthed.

Stepping to the side, I saw it was Kha she was speaking to.

"Girl, stop. Come in, Kha," I told him and shot her a look.

Naomi grilled him as he bypassed her and walked into the apartment. She then followed suit and entered as well.

"Who's this?" she asked as if he wasn't standing right in front of both of us.

"Ain't none of your business, shorty. You drawn," Kha answered.

"Indigo!" She rolled her eyes at him and looked at me.

I rubbed my temple. "This is Quest's folks. Why is yo' ass all hyper?"

"Nah, because he pulled up like he owned the place or something." She looked him up and down.

"Aye, Indigo. Let me holla at you for a minute," Kha intervened.

"Come." I motioned for him to follow me to the back of the apartment. "Wassup?

"I got a message from Quest. He wanted me to come here and grab some things from his room for him," he informed me.

"Oh, okay. Did he mention anything about me?" I wondered.

Kha shook his head no and gave me a sympathetic look. "Nah."

"Okay." I quickly blinked away the tears I felt beginning to well. "Go ahead, it's this room," I showed him, then went back to the living room to meet Naomi, who was on the couch curled up on her phone. She eyed me when I sat down but didn't say a word.

A couple of minutes later, Kha walked out with a bookbag on his shoulder. "Ard, I'm out."

I jumped up off the couch and walked up to him. "Is he still at PICC?" I inquired.

"Yeah. The lawyer went to see him today, so be on the lookout for a call from him. His name is Cohen. He needs to talk to you," he disclosed.

"Okay, no problem."

"Ard. Be good. Call me if anything," he stated before walking out the door.

I closed and locked the door behind him, then returned to the living room.

"Now, he is fine as shit," Naomi blurted out.

I side-eyed her. "Girl, leave that man alone. Don't you have a boo?"

"And do, but I ain't married." She raised up her ring finger. "I could smell a gangsta from miles away." She smirked.

"Lord, you need help." I got up and walked to the kitchen. "Let me feed my baby."

THE WEEKEND HAD PASSED, AND I WAS ANXIOUS for Monday to arrive. After doing some research on the facility Quest was located at, I saw I needed to schedule a visit before going. The requirement was to schedule it online forty-eight hours in advance, so I did just that. I also had an audiologist appointment the same day, so I scheduled the visit for afterward during the three to four o'clock slots they had.

Stepping out of my car, I made my way inside the medical facility as the cool winds blew through my long hair. When I got inside, I noticed it wasn't a busy day, so I would've been in and out. I checked in at the receptionist's desk and was told to fill out some forms. It took me about five minutes to complete it and hand it back in. Then it was a waiting game.

After about a half an hour wait, I was called back to see the audiologist. They made me repeat the same test I had done at the doctor's office. With the headphones in my ear and the sticks with the buttons to press in my hands, I pressed down on them when I heard something. The test went on for about twenty minutes before we completed it, and the audiologist sat down to review my results.

"Okay, so it looks like you are experiencing rapid hearing loss. Judging from the results from your initial test at your doctor's that prompted you to come here, things have gotten worse," she explained.

My ears started to tingle as I felt myself getting emotional.

"Are you serious?" I asked in disbelief. "So, what's going to happen to me?"

"We need to get you a hearing aid." She started to look at the paperwork in my folder. "Do you have insurance?"

Oh God, I thought as I hung my head.

I did have insurance, but it was through Malachi's job. After leaving him, he made sure to remove me from his family plan.

"No, I don't, unfortunately."

"Without insurance, a hearing aid could cost you anywhere around a thousand to ten thousand dollars. It depends on the brand, technology, and features. I suggest getting something affordable for now until you can get something better. We just need to get you one before it's too late."

I nodded. "I understand. Please let me know how much it will cost, and I'll work on getting the money."

Being that Quest was away, and I had to handle all the bills, I wasn't sure how the hell I was going to come up with that much money to get the hearing aid. Stress immediately started to consume me.

"Okay, great."

She gave me a new date to come back as we wrapped our appointment up. As I was leaving the building, I looked at the time on my phone and saw it was 2:33 p.m. Checking ahead of time, I knew the medical office and the prison were twenty minutes away from each other. I hopped in my car and made my way over to Philadelphia Industrial Correctional Center to see my man, hoping he cheered me up after receiving the news I did.

WHEN I GOT TO THE FACILITY, I FOUND PARKING on the street and walked to the main entrance on State

Road. A lot of people were making their way into the building, which told me that visiting was going to be crowded. I followed the lead of others since it looked like they'd been there before.

After waiting patiently in line, I finally reached the guard's desk to give both my and Quest's information for the visit.

"Hi, who are you here to visit?" a woman CO asked.

"Quesnel MacQuoid," I spelled out his name for her.

"Can I have your ID?" she requested.

I handed her over my ID and waited patiently for her to finish doing what she was doing. After a few moments, she handed me back my ID. "Continue to the waiting room," she instructed.

Again, I followed what everyone else was doing. I watch them place their belongings away in a locker, including their phones and jewelry. The only thing we were allowed to have was a clear Ziplock bag with money in it for the vending machines. I read this up online and was happy to know I was prepared.

Once all of my belongings were put away, I went through the security procedures. It was my first time visiting anyone in prison or jail, so being touched all over in a search was uncomfortable, to say the least. The woman guard literally grabbed my coochie and felt up my breasts. If I wasn't dying to see my baby, I would've about-face and never returned. Walking out of the search room, I saw another waiting room. Right before entering the visiting floor, we had to check in with another set of officers.

"What's the name of the inmate?" a male CO inquired.

"Quesnel MacQuoid," I answered.

"Okay, have a seat, and we'll call you."

I took a seat and watched as different people's names were being called, and they went inside to see their loved ones.

As the minutes passed, my stomach became uneasy. I tried to visualize how our visit was going to go. *Was he going to be happy to see me? Was he going to be upset with me? Would he hug and kiss me or just sit down?* My mind wandering started to drive me insane.

An hour passed, and I was still sitting there. People who came after me had already gone inside and came back out. That's when I knew something wasn't right, so I went to the guard's desk and inquired.

"Hi, I've been here for over an hour, and you haven't called my name," I mentioned.

"Who's the inmate?" a woman asked. The guy who was there before left.

"Quesnel MacQuoid," I answered.

She jumped on the phone and spoke with someone.

After a brief exchange, she hung up and shot me a sadistic look. "He has refused your visit. I'm sorry."

Those words hit me like a ton of bricks, and I felt my heart break in half. *How could he do this to me?*

Before a tear dropped, I quickly thanked her and rushed out of the room. I moved swiftly back to the lockers to retrieve my belongings, then left out of the building. Fighting to hold in my tears, I briskly walked to my car and hopped in. Once in the privacy of my vehicle, I broke down crying like never before.

I felt my heart beating outside of my chest at a rapid pace. My body temperature rose, making me hotter than I already was. Sickness came down on me as I felt what I ate quickly coming back up. I opened the car door and threw up everything I had in me.

This can't be it. Why me?

NAIM "NAI" DAVIS

"Shit just don't be adding up, Naim," Naomi fussed.

There I was, tryna get some pussy, and all she wanted to do was nag and complain about me not spending enough time with her and a bunch of other shit.

"Nomi, come on with this. You know a nigga be out on them streets getting to it. What's the fuckin' problem?"

"That's cool and all, Naim, but why you can't answer your phone? And then you don't even call back. I still have to blow up your phone after you done seen me call you how many times. If you don't want this, I'm cool with that." She stood with her hands on her hips in front of me.

I threw my head back on the couch and sighed out loud. Naomi was blowing my high on every level known to mind kind. There was enough shit in the streets I had to worry about. I didn't need any additional headaches, especially with a couple of bricks and over a hundred thousand missing.

"Naomi, shit is just a bit hectic right now. I'm deep in some shit I'm trying to clear up. I really need you to be a nigga peace right now, not a headache," I plead.

"Don't do that. I hate it when you try to switch shit up and make me feel bad or feel like I'm stressing you. You know you're on bullshit, nigga. Quiet pla—"

Her phone started to ring in her hand. When she looked at it, she answered the call, and whoever it was had to have been very important to her for her to answer while she was drawn on me.

"Hey, how was it?" she quickly answered.

Naomi listened to the person for a few seconds before responding. "Hold on, wait, wait. Slow down, Indigo. What do you mean you couldn't see him?" She started to listen some more. "He refused the visit? What? Where are you?" There was a brief silence while she listened, and I looked on. "I'm coming now." She finally hung up.

"Where the hell are you going? We ain't even finished here, and my balls are still full!" I angrily blurted out.

"Seriously, Naim?"

"I'm dead ass serious, Naomi."

"My friend needs me," she voiced.

"And yo' nigga needs you. The fuck? Anyway, who the hell is this Indigo chick I keep hearing about? I don't even know what the bitch looks like in case some shit was to happen to you."

"What's gon' happen to me, Naim? And you never asked to meet her."

"Because I don't want to. I just wanna know who the fuck she is."

For all I knew, it was just another nigga in her life she was tryna skate off with. I could admit that I wasn't the best at the whole boyfriend thing. I was knee-deep in the streets and was still fuckin' around with a bunch of bitches. They didn't measure up to Naomi, though, but I just still wasn't a hundred percent ready to be fully committed.

"Here, this is her." She showed me a picture of the jawn on her phone. And it so happened to be Quest's bitch. I had to hold my composure and not show my hand. "You happy now?" she grumbled.

"Yeah, ard, whatever." I waved her off. "Go console your little friend. I'ma go make a move, anyway." I stood to my feet.

Naomi smacked her lips and rolled her eyes at me before walking out of the living room. I made my way to the door, then out to my whip. When I got in, I started it up right away and made a block, parking up on the corner where she'd have to pass since her block was a one-way street.

Since she was going to see Ms. Indigo, I made up my mind to go follow her and see where the bitch was. Word on the street was Quest had gotten locked up again for violating probation, so there was no telling where my money and bricks were. Still, if I had some kind of leverage against him, there was a possibility I could get my shit back.

Ten minutes had passed before Naomi hopped in her car and drove off. I pulled out two cars behind and followed her lead. We drove for about fifteen minutes before I peeped her pull into a parking spot. I stopped abruptly and parked in the first spot I saw. Cutting the engine, I watched her get out of her car and enter into a newly built building.

I had no idea what apartment she went into and how long it was going to be before neither of them exited the building. Waiting around was not an option for me, so I called up one of my young bulls and dropped my location for him to pull up on me. He took about half an hour to get to me, and during that time, the ladies hadn't moved.

After explaining to him what I needed him to do, which was to keep an eye on the building for when the jawn came out. I went onto Naomi's Instagram, which I hardly did because I didn't follow her, and I was barely on social media to see if she had any pictures with Indigo. It was just my luck that she did, so I showed my young'n how she looked and sent him the picture afterward. Once he was situated, I dipped to go meet Ak. We had to link the plug.

HOURS LATER, I MADE MY WAY OVER THE BEN Franklin Bridge to a meeting I was dreading for some time. When I got the last-minute text from Ak saying we had to go and see Black, my mind started to wander almost immediately.

Black was our plug and someone not to be fucked with. The nigga was ruthless and had not one care in the world. He killed one of his workers for getting the wrong food order. Another time, he killed another nigga for stepping on his sneakers. They were only white Air Forces. He was manic as it got.

When I arrived at the studio he owned in Camden, New Jersey, I saw Ak's Benz parked outside. Parking right next to him, I noticed he was still inside of the car on the phone. I cut my engine, removed my Glock from my waist, and placed it under the seat. Weapons weren't allowed in the building. Only Black's people carried them.

I slid out of my car and knocked on his window. Moments later, he hung up with whoever it was he was talking to and got out of the vehicle.

"'Bout time yo' ass got here." Ak slammed his door.

"Nigga, I don't control the fuckin' traffic," I shot back.

"What the fuck is yo' ass was doing, anyway?" He eyed me.

"I'll tell you later. Why the fuck do you think we're here?" We started to walk toward the entrance of the building.

"What else? He probably wanna know where the fuck we been."

After the spot got hit about two months back, for bricks and the money, we were dry in the streets. That was a fresh new re-up, and the money was supposed to go toward an even bigger order than we ever had done.

We shot each other a knowing look and continued our way inside. Black's guards met us at the entrance, searched us, then led us upstairs to where he was. Walking into the studio he occupied, he first didn't pay us any attention when we walked in. He just carried on bopping his head to the music that was playing.

After a few more minutes of the song playing, it finally went off.

"Big Ak, King Nai," he called out our full street names. "How y'all niggas been?"

Ak raised his hands. "I'm alive, can't complain," Ak answered.

Black nodded with a smile, then looked at me.

"Staying low and out of the way."

"Mmm, yeah, y'all staying low, ard." He stood up from his seat and walked toward us.

We both stood there with our heads up and chest out.

"I thought y'all were copping a large order? What about a month ago? What happened to that?" He leaned against the island it had in the middle of the studio floor.

"We're still situating some shit," Ak started.

"You're still situating some shit," Black mocked and nodded his head. "You talkin' 'bout that hit on your spot?"

Ak and I looked at one another. Black knew every single thing that went down in the tri-state area, especially Philly. We were better off just communicating with him from the jump when it first happened. I suggested it, but Ak said it would've made us look weak and that we needed to handle it first and then let him know what happened.

"We're going to straighten things out and still cop the weight," Ak assured him.

"You damn right you will because I'm sitting on fuckin' more bricks than I need, all because you requested it. Y'all got a month to bring me my money." He turned around and pointed at the engineer to play the music.

That was our cue to get the fuck up out of there before he felt we overstayed our welcome and blew our fuckin' heads off just because.

When we got outside to the cars, Ak and I stood there in silence for a moment. That's when I remembered I put my young on the one lead we had to get back our money and weight. That was if niggas hadn't already spent it and sold the drugs.

When my workers at the spot described the people who bussed in, I already knew it was Quest. He was a big ass nigga whose height and size were hard to ignore. In the beginning, I wanted the shit to not be true, but after questioning all of them time after time after time, their stories never changed, and they all sounded alike.

"I'm gon' kill that nigga," Ak randomly blurted out.

"We gotta get that shit back, ASAP," I added. "You wouldn't believe the shit that dropped in my lap today."

"What?"

"My bitch is cool with Quest's bitch. I followed my jawn to her spot, but I left the lil' nigga Meen there to track her," I informed him.

"Nigga, next time, lead with this kind of information. The fuck."

"My fault, nigga."

"Pull up on that bitch. Since he's not out here, he'd do whatever to protect her, which would be to give up our shit."

"Word, that makes sense. You think he knows who set him up and killed his fam?" I quizzed.

Ak looked into the air, then back at me. "I'm almost positive his eyes are on us, so Whatever he wanna do, I'm for it."

"Fuckin' with his bitch, he really gon' be on bullshit when he gets out."

"Then so be it. We just gon' be on even heavier bullshit." He shrugged, then got in his car.

Ak started up his whip and pulled out of the parking spot. Speeding off, his tires skid on the concrete, leaving smoke in the air. When the smoke cleared, it was just me standing there, something I believed was going to happen when shit hit the roof — me facing shit on my own.

Indigo TAYLOR

A few days had passed since I attempted to visit Quest. My emotions were all over the place, and I felt unsure of what would happen to me. My entire world was crashing down on top of me. I was pregnant and constantly sick, my child's father wanted nothing to do with me, the one person I was starting to resent and despise wouldn't leave me alone, and I was losing my hearing. Life was a complete wreck, and I didn't know what to do.

While I just wanted to curl up and stay in bed, eat junk food, watch TV, and cry all day, I didn't have the luxury of that. Rent was due, and bills still had to be paid, or I would end up back in the same predicament as when I first met Quest. Still, through everything, I tried my hardest to place my feelings on the back burner and do what I had to do.

"Indigo, you can go to lunch now," my supervisor informed me.

I quickly locked my computer and grabbed my bag from the drawer. My co-worker would handle the front desk while I went to eat, and when I was finished, I'd do the same for her.

As I was making my way upstairs, my phone rang, but I didn't recognize the number. Hoping it was Quest, I answered the call.

"Hello?"

"Hi, good afternoon. Is this Indigo Taylor?" a man inquired.

"Yes, it is. Who's asking?" I raised a brow.

"I'm Mr. Cohen, Quesnel's attorney," he revealed.

My eyes opened wide, and my heart started racing, thinking something was wrong.

"How may I help you?"

"I need to speak with you regarding Quesnel's case. Is now a good time, or would you rather you come into my office for us to speak face-to-face?"

"Honestly, there's a lot going on right now, and I'd have to confirm whether you are his lawyer. From what I remember, the person who represented Quesnel was a guy named Thomas."

"His friend Khaleef referred me to take over Quesnel's case."

Once I heard Kha's name, then I knew he was legit. I just needed to be sure because Malachi was a weird, sneaky kind of person.

"Oh, yes. Since you mentioned his friend's name, I now feel comfortable talking to you."

We started discussing some things in Quest's case, which had everything to do with me. Cohen requested I send him proof of my marriage to Malachi and proof of my relationship with Quest. Once I revealed to him that I was indeed carrying Quest's child, he suggested I get paperwork from my doctor proving my pregnancy as well. He assured me once we had all of this, he could file the appeal with the evidence, and Quest should be released.

"Please send these things to me at your earliest convenience. I will shoot you a text message of the email to send it to as soon as we hang up."

"How long would this take?" I inquired before letting him go.

"Once I file it, it can take anywhere from a week to six months. There's no set time. Let's just pray they pick it up as soon as I rest it down."

"Okay, I understand. Thanks for calling. I will send over everything in a little while."

"Great. Have a great day. Speak to you soon."

"You as well."

I took it as a sign that God was working. Cohen called just when I was going to lunch and had all the time to email him over everything. Luckily for me, I always took pictures and saved them in a document album of everything important, such as my birth certificate, social security card, marriage certificate, and things of those sorts. The new doctor I visited had an online portal where patients could log on and find their recent labs and results. I grabbed the one with my pregnancy test results and downloaded it.

Once I was comfortable in the break room, I warmed up my lunch, then sat down and started to search for everything he requested. I ate my meal and felt a slight weight lifted off my shoulders now that things were looking up for Quest after the phone call from the lawyer.

Most people would've been embarrassed about the situation, especially having to submit such things that could possibly paint me in a negative light. However, at that point, I didn't care what I looked like in other people's eyes. I knew who I was. Plus, I would've done anything to get Quest out of prison.

The remainder of the day went by smoothly. I started to feel better after I ate lunch and my mind was at ease just a little. When four o'clock rolled around, I gathered my things and clocked out of work.

Stepping outside of the building onto the busyness of Broad Street, the sun was still beaming. The spring weather made the place feel light. I happily walked to my car, which I parked around the corner on Cherry Street. As I approached it, I heard a voice behind me.

"Where yo' nigga at?" a man asked.

It sounded just like another man trying to holla at me, so I paid it no mind. Instead of turning around, I just unlocked my car and was about to climb in my seat through open the door until it was shut from behind.

I turned around with the quickness. "Bitch, I asked you where yo' nigga at?" he angrily grilled.

My heart dropped into my ass when I saw it was the same dude, Naim, that had the gun pointed at Quest at the shop. Quest had given me a brief rundown of their relationship. Naim was once his best friend, but things changed once Quest went inside. And at that point, they were newfound enemies.

"Please, leave me alone," I calmly told him.

My heart tripled in speed, but I kept a poker face on.

"Ask Quest where the fuck my shit is. Until I get back

what's mine, I will keep paying you a visit, Indigo," he threatened.

"I don't know what you're talking about. Just leave me out of this." I turned to open the door, but he tightly gripped hold of my arm.

I tried snatching my arm away from him, but it was no good. He had a firm grip on me. Panic started to consume me because I wasn't sure what he would do next. From what Quest told me, Naim was a dangerous person.

Looking at his lips, I knew he was saying something, but I couldn't hear him. My hearing went away, and I started to feel sick. Two men walking past approached us, which made Naim let go of my arm. Before I knew it, he walked off, and the two guys made sure I got into my car.

Rattled to the core, I started my car and recklessly pulled off. I was so shook and paranoid that I kept looking in my rearview mirror to see if anyone was following me. Going home was not an option, and going to Naomi couldn't help me, so the only option I had left was to go to the tire shop to see Kha.

On my way to him, I called, but it was pointless. My hearing still hadn't returned, so I knew I was rambling on in fear. If he asked me a question, I didn't even know what it was. I started to cry hysterically because I was so frightened by the whole situation, then I couldn't hear to save my fuckin' life.

Blinking away my tears to clear my blurred vision, I drove fast through the Philly streets. It took me about twenty minutes to get to Broad and Olney. When I turned down the block and pulled up at the shop, I saw Kha outside, waiting. I didn't even shut off the engine. I just got out and ran to him. He wrapped his arms around me tightly and held my head.

Kha took me inside and into his office, sat me down, and gave me a bottle of water. He sat down in front of me, and thankfully, I slowly started to hear his voice.

"Calm down, Indi. Calm down," he coached.

One of his workers came into the office and handed him my keys before he quickly reverted his attention to me.

"What happened?" Kha questioned, leaning over with his forearms on his thighs.

I took a deep breath in and let it out. "The bull, Naim," I started.

"Okay, what about him?" He squinted his eyes.

"He approached me when I was getting in my car. He said if Quest doesn't give him back what belongs to him, he'll keep paying me a visit," I explained.

Kha sat back in his seat and ran his hands down his face.

"And he put his hands on me. Thank God for two guys passing. They got him to let go of my arm," I added.

"What?" Kha jumped up and roared.

He started to pace the office floor back and forth. I could tell the mention of Naim overly grabbing me bothered him.

"Don't worry, I'll handle it," he assured me. "In the meantime, I'ma put you in an Airbnb until shit calms down. I'll go with you home to pack some stuff. Ard?"

I nodded in agreement. It sounded like a safe thing to do. Besides, I don't think I had a choice. Quest wasn't home, so my next option of staying safe was his friend.

Damn, I need you, Q, I thought to myself.

QUESNEL
Quest MACQUOID

"**D**addy!" Kaedon screamed.

"I'm coming, my boy, I'm coming!" I reassured him.

"Baby, hurry up. It's so hot!" my mother cried.

"Daddy!" Kaedon hollered.

Bang. Bang. Bang.

"Wake up!" a guard hollered as if I was miles away, snatching me from my nightmare. Although he startled me, I was grateful for him waking me up.

I turned around to see him just standing there at the cell door. After the fight, they placed me in the hole. While I hated to be in such a small space because a nigga was big, I took it as a blessing to be away from everyone. I wasn't sure who else would've tried to get at me for that nut-ass nigga, Anderson.

"Fuck I'm gettin' up for?" I questioned.

"Legal visit... unless you don't want it," he retorted.

If it were one visit that I would never turn down, it was one from my lawyer. On the other hand, I had to refuse the visit from Indigo. I wasn't ready to see her. Everything was just so fresh, and to top things off, her husband damn near sent a hit out on me. What the fuck I looked like sitting up in a visiting room with her?

"Play a safer game, my nigga." I stood up.

"Yeah, yeah. I'll be back in five minutes."

I brushed my teeth, washed my face, and put on my jumpsuit properly. As I was about to sit on my bunk and wait for the guard to return, I heard my cell slot being unlocked.

"Let's go." He motioned for me to get up.

Turning around, I placed my hands behind my back and walked backward to the door. I bent down a little so that my hands aligned with the slot. He put the handcuffs on my wrists and locked it. Once I was restrained, he opened the cell door, took me out, and escorted me to the visiting room to see my lawyer.

When I walked into the room, Cohen looked me up and down as the guard took the handcuffs off of me.

"What's that about?" he questioned.

"I got into a fight and got sent to the hole. It's nuffin'," I assured him.

"Must I remind you that what you do here will affect your appeal?"

"Well, I'm away from everyone now, so I should be straight, right?"

"Right." He shot me a knowing look, then picked up a paper. "I wanted to let you know I spoke with Indigo, and she sent over everything I needed regarding the evidence. I filed the appeal, and now it's a waiting game," he informed me.

I nodded. "Good shit, good shit. How long do you think it'll take?"

"That I can't tell you. It could be tomorrow or six months from now, and you'd already be home."

"Damn," I whispered.

"I've always had luck with getting them seen fast, though, so just keep your fingers crossed and stay out of the way."

"Ard, I got it."

I started to get up to leave, but he stopped me. "I have something to give you." He handed me a letter.

From the jump, I figured it was a letter from Indigo since she couldn't see me on a visit, and I wasn't calling her.

"Nah, I'm good," I declined.

"You need to read it. It's from Khaleef," Cohen informed me.

I quickly grabbed the letter from his hand and opened it.

Q,

I hope you're holding your head up. You're built for anything, my nigga. But look, that goofy pulled up on Indigo, sending threats. He even grabbed and roughed her up a bit. I got her in an Airbnb for now, and I will make sure one of the guys or myself takes her to work and back to where she's staying.

Let me know what to do. I'm waiting on you.

-Kha

STARING STRAIGHT AHEAD AT THE GRAY WALL, I clenched my jaw as I rested the letter on the table. "When did he send this?" I wondered.

"First thing this morning before I left my office to come here," he answered. "But there's more."

I turned and looked at Cohen. "What else?"

Cohen toyed with his hands as if he were trying to find the best way to tell me what he had to tell me. "Indigo is carrying your child," he blurted out.

The room froze, and all noised ceased. My temples

started pounding to the beat of my heart, which was speeding up rapidly.

"Quest?" Cohen called out to me.

"How far is she?" I felt tears threatening to fall, but I blinked them away.

I had been so fucked up to her all while she was going through a pregnancy alone. Then, to hear because of my actions, her life was being threatened triggered something dangerous in me. I know she fucked up not being completely honest with me, but all that shit went out the window when I was informed she was in danger and carrying my seed on top of it.

"She's about two months now. Forgive me if I'm wrong."

Two months? I asked myself.

I thought back to the day she wanted to talk to me. She told me about the hearing loss, then said she had some other things she wanted to let me know. I wondered if she knew she was pregnant then, and that's what she had to tell me. I also speculated if she had planned to open up and tell me about her marriage situation. My mind was going wild with different thoughts.

"Good lookin', Cohen," I told him.

"What should I tell Khaleef?" he asked as he stood up.

"Tell him to hold it down. I'm coming home. Just make sure Indigo and my baby are safe."

He nodded. "Alright, I will. Be safe, and I'll see you soon." He walked out of the room.

Moments later, the guard came back into the room and cuffed me. As we were making our way back to the hole, I asked him if I could make a phone call.

"You only get one call a week," he informed me.

"Ard."

He placed me back in my cell and walked off to get the phone. Not long after, I heard a cart being rolled down the long hallway before stopping in front of my door. The guard opened the slot and asked me the number to dial. I didn't know Indigo's number by heart, so I gave him Kha's number, hoping he was with her or for him to call her on three-way.

"You got five minutes." He handed me the phone and walked off.

I listened as the phone rang.

"Hello?" Kha answered.

"Bro, it's Quest."

"My nigga, you good?"

"Yeah, I'm straight. You around Indi?"

"Nah, she's at work."

"Call her on three-way real quick. I don't have a lot of time."

He didn't even utter another word as he went and did

what I asked. A few seconds later, he clicked back on the line, and I heard her voice.

"Kha, I'm at work, I'll call you when—"

"Indigo," I called out, cutting her off.

"Qu-Quest?" she stuttered.

"Yeah."

The line went silent as I heard her cry. It broke a nigga's heart knowing she was going through so much without me.

"Shhh, shhh. Don't cry, Chunks."

"I miss you so much," she whispered.

"I miss you, too, baby girl. I'll be home soon, ard?"

"Mmm-hmmm." She continued to cry.

"I just needed to hear your pretty voice." She giggled.

"Alright, MacQuoid! It's time!" the guard shouted as he walked down the hall toward me.

"Aye, Kha," I called him.

"Yo?"

"Pull up on me ASAP. Bring her with you," I instructed.

"Ard, say no more."

"I gotta go, y'all. I love you, Indigo."

She sniffled. "I love you more, Quesnel."

I hung up just as the guard reached me.

Fuck!

The way I was feeling, I could've killed anyone that

spoke to me wrong. Hearing I was having another child after losing one many years ago gave a nigga hope. Before my son or daughter came into the world, I wanted to make sure I had all issues resolved and all loose ends tied up. That included Naim's snake ass and Ak for setting me up and killing my family. That also included Indigo's situation with her husband. I needed to have a serious talk with her to have a better understanding of what the fuck was going on and what her plans were.

"Chow!" the guard yelled.

I was pacing my cell floor when the chow cart made it to my door. The slot was opened, and an inmate slid a tray inside. When I picked it up, a note fell on the ground. I stepped on the note until the CO closed the slot and walked off. Once it was safe, I rested my tray on the metal table and picked up the note.

Don't eat the food.

I looked at the note and scrunched my face up. It didn't take me long to figure out what was being warned of me. The food had poisoning in it, or they messed with it. Inmates were in charge of cooking the populations meals. They also delivered them to the units with the escort of a CO, so the inmate who gave me my tray had to have seen or heard something in order for him to pass me such a note.

It had Anderson's or even Naim's and Ak's names

written all over that shit. First, it was the niggas on the unit who jumped me. Now, they went further to get at me while I was locked away.

I looked over at the tray of food, which was sloppy joe, bread, and salad. I took the milk that was on there and ate the closed crackers. When the cart came back around, I slid that bitch out damn near how it came in. I made a mental note to grab some things from the commissary when I could shop. Then again, I prayed I didn't get a chance to shop and just got released instead. I had to get the fuck out of there and to my folks. Shit was getting real scary.

Indigo TAYLOR

"Indigo," my co-worker, Angel, called out to me.

I snapped my head at her. "Yeah, sorry."

"Is everything okay?" she pried.

I was still on cloud nine from hearing Quest's voice. After he acted like he wanted nothing to do with me, I thought that was it for us. I would be lying if I said I didn't know what had gotten into him. The bull Naim pulling up on me definitely had a huge part to play in things. I also had a feeling someone told him about the baby because that man became hella soft. I heard it in his voice.

"Yeah, I'm good. Sorry, I was just zoned out, thinking about something."

"Or someone." She eyed me with a smirk.

"Yeah, definitely that." We both giggled until we saw someone walking up to the front desk.

Quickly getting back into work mode, I kept checking the time to see if it was time to clock out. I wanted to get out of there so I could schedule the visit for Kha and myself. My anxiety level was rising to the roof with thoughts of finally seeing him, although it had only been like two weeks since he's been gone. I just wanted to be in my man's skin.

Most would say I was dumb for fully accepting Quest's behavior toward me, but the mature folks would understand it was love. Plus, I played a part in a lot of things. I just wanted us to resolve all our issues and move forward. Quest was who I wanted to be with, while Malachi was my past.

Four o'clock finally rolled around, and it was time to go. I grabbed my things and made my way for the door right after clocking out. The moment I stepped foot outside, I saw Saleem standing close to the entrance. When he saw me, he smiled and gave me a little wave. I looked down the street and saw Razor sitting in the car, looking around.

Earlier that morning, Kha drove me to work and told me that the guys were going to be there by the time I got off. He assured me that until the smoke cleared, there would always be someone with me, at least until Quest came home.

"You good?" Saleem asked as he walked up to me.

"Yeah." I shot him a faint smile.

"Ard." We started walking toward the car. "You got anywhere you gotta go besides going back to the apartment?" he inquired.

"I just want to grab something to e—"

My words were cut short when I saw Naim driving by in a Charger. His window was down, and he was staring directly at me. Saleem followed my eyes and saw him, immediately pulling his gun out of his waistband.

Bypassers saw the gun and started to run and scream while Naim sped off and bent the corner.

"Come on." Saleem placed his hand on my upper back and quickly rushed me to the car.

Once we got in, Razor pulled off, and we headed to meet Kha.

Two days had passed since the little scare with Naim driving by. I was glad the guys were there when it happened, so they were a witness to the craziness that nigga was on. When we met with Kha, he took me to the

Airbnb while Saleem and Razor went and got me some Chipotle.

Kha calmed me down and talked to me about everything. Once my head leveled, I went online and scheduled a visit for both of us to see Quest. After I ate, and he felt I was okay to be alone, he left but kept checking in periodically.

"You ready?" Kha asked.

I was staring outside the car window, watching the buildings and other vehicles go by. We were on our way to the prison to see Quest. Since he called the other day, we hadn't received another call from him, so Kha called his lawyer, and that's when we found out he was in the hole. When they were in the hole, most of their privileges were stripped, which explained the very brief call he had when I first spoke to him.

"Yeah." I nodded and smiled, although I was a nervous wreck deep down inside.

Walking into that place, I didn't know what to expect as far as my surroundings and from Quest. I just prayed it would be a smooth visit for all of us.

We had finally arrived at PICC. Kha found a parking spot on the street not too far from the entrance. We exited the car and anxiously made our way to the entrance. There weren't that many people there like it was when I first went there.

Unbeknownst to me, Kha had already been there many times, as a visitor and as an inmate, so he already knew the procedure. We checked in with the guards, went through the first security checkpoint, put our things away in the locker, went through the intense search, and finally, we made it onto the visiting floor.

We waited for about five minutes for Quest to come out. When I saw his huge build come through a door that looked to be too small for him to fit, my eyes widened at the sight of him. Quest was the most handsome man I'd ever met. And although he wasn't in total control of his life or surroundings, he walked like he owned the place. It was clear as day he was no regular ass nigga. Even a blind person could've seen that.

Kha and I stood to our feet as he got closer. Once in front of us, Quest gently grabbed me by the waist, pulling me in for a hug and kissing me on my head. He then dapped up Kha as they embraced each other before we all sat down.

"What's the word?" Kha asked Quest as soon as his ass touched the seat.

"He's gotta get dealt with, but I wanna be the one to do it," Quest voiced.

"I feel you... as you should," Kha agreed. "In the meantime, I'll just continue to do what I'm doing and make sure Indi's cool until you touch."

"Solid, bro."

"What do you want me to do with those two packages?" I listened to them, not knowing what the hell they were talking about.

"Go ahead and get them off. That fuck nigga's not gettin' shit back anyway," Quest grilled.

"Ard, say no more. I'ma let y'all wrap." The guys stood up and dapped each other up. "I'll be in the waiting room," Kha turned and told me before walking off to exit the visiting room.

Once Quest and I were alone, my heart doubled its speed with anxiety. I looked around the visiting room and saw everyone slowly fading, leaving just Quest in my vision.

"Tell me everything, and don't leave shit out," Quest demanded as he leaned back in his seat and crossed his big ass arms.

I shifted in my seat and started toying with my fingers. It was something I did when I was nervous. Taking a deep breath in, then letting it out, I told myself just to let it all out. That was my chance to make things right so we could move on in the right direction.

Quest looked me straight into my eyes, never blinking. He was intimidating and made me nervous. However, I knew he was as serious as a heart attack, so I put my big girl panties on and started talking. I started from the start, explaining to him Malachi and my marriage and how and why I left. I also revealed that my divorce was in progress.

Quest listened, never taking his eyes off me or moving an inch. When I was finished talking, it was silence between the two of us for a few minutes. I knew he was processing everything and thinking before he spoke.

"Yo' man's sent niggas after me in here. Twice at that," he finally spoke up and revealed.

"He did what?" my eyes bulged. "Are you sure it was him?"

"Positive," he answered. "I'm letting you know now. I cannot promise you I won't see him when I get out."

If I had any ounce of love or care for Malachi, I would've spoken against Quest doing anything to him. However, after everything he'd put me through, then making my life miserable with the person I wanted to be with, I couldn't care. Whatever Quest wanted to do, that was on him because even if I said not to, Quest was a grown ass man who made his own decisions. I just didn't want to know when, why, how, or when it went down.

I shrugged. "That's on you, baby," I nonchalantly mentioned.

He nodded, then leaned forward. "Indigo, you should have told me all this from the jump. You may not have had to go into detail about what you went through just yet, but I should've known you were married when we decided to take things to the next level."

"You're right. I'm so sorry," I apologized.

"If I had known, we could've put two and two together and knew my PO was your husband. Nonetheless, everything has happened now, so we can't cry over spilled milk. I just need to know where your head is and where your loyalty lies."

"That shouldn't even be a question, Quest. I'm with you," I assured him.

"Ard, I hear you. Now tell me about this baby." He leaned back and smiled while sizing me up and down.

I giggled like a schoolgirl. "We're having a babyyy..." I sang.

His eyes became glossy, letting me know he got emotional. Quest had a very hard exterior, so for him to crack even a little, I knew he really cared for me.

Before anyone noticed, he quickly blinked away any tears trying to escape. "I'm 'bout to be a whole father again," he stated in a whisper.

I nodded and smiled at him. "And I'm about to be a mommy for the first time."

Since he was already on edge about Malachi, I kept the fine details of what Malachi said about the baby being his to myself for the time being. When the time was right, and Quest was home, I would fill him in on things.

I knew certain the baby was Quest's because of the timeframe. Malachi and I hadn't had sex in a while. Before I left, we were intimate once about a month before, so the timing was off. Of course, Malachi didn't know how far I was, and I felt I didn't have to tell him shit. I was confident who the daddy was, and that's all that mattered to me.

Quest and I spoke some more until the guards announced visitation was over. The energy and vibe definitely shifted once I told him everything and poured my heart out. The guilt, sad, and worried feeling I had walking into the prison was no longer there.

"I'm coming home soon, and on my soul, I won't allow anything to happen to you and my baby. If a nigga inhales your scent, I'm knocking his head off, so far less for him putting his hands on you," Quest threatened. "I love you, Indigo. Don't make me regret doing so."

Tears fell down my cheeks. "I won't, I promise. I love you more, Quesnel."

"Let's go! Visitation is over. Say goodbye to your loved ones. Visitors stay seated until the inmates have exited," a guard announced.

As we stood to our feet, Quest grabbed me close and tight as our lips connected. A whole wave of shock ran through my body at his touch, especially knowing we were back good. I didn't want to let him go, but I knew it wasn't an option at the time.

"MacQuoid, let's go!" the guard yelled.

Quest pecked my lips once more before walking away. Watching him leave made me emotional as shit, but I knew it wasn't a forever thing. Before passing the threshold back into their world, he turned around and shot me a wink, making me blush and melt. I loved my man, and it wasn't anything in the world that was going to break us apart.

RING. RING.

I jumped out of my sleep when I heard my phone ringing. Quest was the first person who came to mind who could've been on the other side of the line. When I grabbed my phone and saw it was Kha, disappointment washed over me, but I answered.

"Good morning," I greeted him.

"Morning, sis. I need you to get up and get yourself ready," he instructed.

"For what?"

It was a Saturday, which meant I was off. Sleeping in was something I loved to do on the weekends, so I wasn't sure what he had going on.

"Stop asking questions and get ready," he demanded.

Kha wouldn't have taken me anywhere that I wasn't safe and wouldn't do anything that Quest didn't approve of, so I gave in.

I sighed out loud. "Okayyy!" I rolled my eyes as if he could see.

"I'll be there to get you in an hour."

"Mmm-hmm." We hung up.

Before I rolled out of bed, I checked my phone to see if I had any missed calls or messages. I had one from Naomi, one from SHEIN, and another from Fashion Nova. I responded to Naomi, then made my way to the bathroom to handle my cleanliness. Within the hour given, I was dressed and ready to go.

Promptly, there was a knock on the door of the Airbnb. Looking through the peephole, I saw Kha standing there with roses, so I quickly swung open the door.

"What's all this?" I quizzed.

He didn't answer me. Instead, he just smiled and handed me a note. It read:

Chunks,
Just a little something to let you know that I love and care about you.
-Quest

Tears immediately started to fall as I heard his voice while reading the quick note. What made me more emotional was the fact I didn't see it coming. It was the small things that drew me to Quest in the first place. Although he had me, he kept applying pressure and showing that he wanted to keep me.

"Come on, I gotta take you somewhere." Kha handed me the bouquet of roses.

I sniffed the beautifully scented roses and left out of the Airbnb. Kha locked up since he had a spare key, and then we headed to his Range Rover.

On the way to the unknown destination, he blasted music while I enjoyed the ride and thought about Quest. We drove for about half an hour before pulling into a parking lot. When I looked closely, I saw we were at a spa called Heyday Plymouth Meeting.

"Spa day?" I asked with a smile.

He nodded and smirked. "Come on."

I slid out of the Range and followed him inside. While Kha spoke with the receptionist, I looked around the place and took in the beautiful and calm scenery. The smell was sweet but not over the top. The music was soft jazz, and the place was clean.

"Indigo, please come with me," the receptionist instructed, grabbing my attention.

I looked at Kha, who motioned for me to go ahead. "I'll be back, ard?"

"Okay." I nodded and went to the back with the woman.

After all that I'd been through in the past few months, I deserved that spa day. I had planned to let my mind relax and enjoy the treatment that was being given to me.

The masseuse handled my body perfectly. I was a bit hesitant at first when I saw how slim and petite she was, but her looks were deceiving. She knew exactly how to relax my body with her hands.

Aside from the full body massage, I received a facial, manicure, pedicure, and wax for all the appropriate areas. I literally got the whole works done, and in the end, I felt like a brand new person.

AFTER SPENDING DAMN NEAR THE ENTIRE DAY there, Kha came back and got me. I told him I was hungry, but instead of taking me to get food, he said we'd order takeout. I wasn't a fussy person, so I just agreed.

When we returned to the Airbnb, I climbed out of his Range, toted my roses up the steps, and waited for him to open the door since my hands were full. As he was unlocking the door, I heard something inside the house.

"What's that?" I looked at him with a worried look.

"What you talkin' 'bout?" he asked, scrunching up his face.

"I heard something." I backed away.

"Man, it ain't nobody in here," Kha assured me, pushing the door open and stepping inside.

I followed right behind, but as soon as I passed the threshold, a delicious smell smacked me in the face. Walking further inside, I saw the place was decorated with balloons, more roses, and some designer boxes from Chanel, Louis Vuitton, and a few other high brands.

Out of nowhere, Naomi popped out of the corner with a wide smile. "Surprise!" she lifted her hands in the air.

My girl ran to me and hugged me tightly.

"What's all this?" I was confused.

Naomi handed me a card. I opened it and read what was inside. It said:

To my lady,
Here's a little something more to express my love. I hope you enjoyed your spa day. Now enjoy your gifts and the private chef.

The best is yet to come…. I'll be home soon. I love you, Chunks.

   -Quest

I stomped my feet like a little child, unable to get my way because everything Quest had was so sweet and meaningful, but all I wanted was him.

"Girl, come open your gifts," Naomi urged.

"Ard, ard. Damn." I fake-acted like I was running excitedly, making Kha and Naomi laugh. She was trying to get me to open gifts when I was more interested in what was cooking in the kitchen.

If only Quest were here to be my dessert.

KHALEEF "KHA" AMIN JR.

"Y'all can do all that girly shit. I want some food," I exclaimed.

I had been running all day to set things up perfectly for Indigo. From getting her to and from the spa, making sure the chef had everything she needed, and helping Naomi with decorations. I also had to go and shop for some things Quest wanted me to get her.

When Cohen called me and relayed the message from Quest, I jumped right into action for my boy. Besides me supporting and helping him out, I sincerely wanted to see both him and Indigo happy. They had and were experiencing a tough time but weren't allowing it to break them apart.

"Exactly! Is the food ready?" Indigo inquired, making

her way to the kitchen while Naomi and I stayed put in the living room.

My phone started to ring, but I ignored it. It was one of my little bitches that I fucked with when I wanted to get my dick wet. After declining her call, she called back again.

"What the fuck?" I let slip out louder than I wanted it to.

I peeped Naomi watching me from the corner of my eye.

"Your hoes calling you?" she pried.

Raising a brow, I started to chuckle. "Yeah, that's exactly what that was," I retorted. "Nosey ass," I mumbled.

"Why you ain't answer then? Does she not know her place?" She giggled.

"She knows her place, just like the rest of them."

"Well, damn. How many are there?" She raised a brow and curled her lip.

"Why do you want to know? You tryna be one of them?"

"Aht-aht, I ain't tryna be nobody's hoe and in their lineup. I'm too good for that, and this pussy should be the only one in the lineup," she sassed.

Naomi was undeniably gorgeous and had a fire body. She was crazy stacked, but her slim frame was proportioned out just right. She had this uppity girl kind of attitude with a hint of ghetto, and for some reason, I was feeling it. I also loved a confident bitch, and that she possessed, something I noticed when we first met outside of Quest and Indigo's apartment.

"You talk heavy, but that'll be something I gotta see for myself." I smirked.

She started to blush. "Fuck around and you won't have a lineup once you see what this is about," she boasted.

"Yeah, that shit sounds good."

"Food's ready!" Indigo yelled from the kitchen, breaking up our little back and forth.

Naomi and I met her and the chef in the dining room, where the chef had set up everything. We were served our meal, and in no time, everyone smashed their plates. With fire food, top-shelf drinks, and good vibes, the evening went well.

After I digested my food and ensured the ladies were good, I left to go and handle some business. However, before I made my exit, I made sure to exchange numbers with Naomi.

Meek Mill's playlist on my phone played in the background while I reviewed inventory. Midnight was my deadline to place my order with my suppliers in order to get everything by a certain date. After dealing with the girls all day, I finally excused myself to head to the tire shop to finalize the order.

The guys ran the shop when I wasn't around. They knew what they had to do and how to do it. Since it was around nine o'clock at night, most of them were gone by the time I arrived. As usual, the only two who stayed back were Saleem and Razor.

Saleem was supposed to make a move for me to sell a brick that Quest had from when we robbed Naim. He knew some young bulls who were getting their feet wet in the game and were buying it for whatever price we laid it out for.

Knock. Knock.

"Yo!" I called out without taking my eyes off the computer screen.

Saleem walked into the office. "What's good?"

Quickly glancing at him, I returned my gaze to the screen. "Shit. I'm doing this order. You ready to make that move?" I raised a brow.

"Yeah. You comin' wit' me?" he inquired.

"You want me to?" I observed his body language.

"Yeah, just in case niggas on some funny shit. I mean, I

know them, but you never know how niggas could get with shit like this," he voiced.

"Ard. Give me a few minutes. I'm almost done."

"Bet."

I finished the order, counted the earnings for the day, and then we locked up to head for the exchange. Razor went along for the drive. The more of us, the safer we were.

THE DROP WAS SCHEDULED FOR MIDNIGHT AT Fairmount Park. We saw a parked car with headlights on as we approached the meeting spot. The surrounding place was dark except for a few working streetlights that weren't bright at all.

When Razor pulled up and came to a stop, I made sure my gun was loaded and ready with one in the chamber. I gave Saleem the green light to go ahead and get out while Razor and I stayed put and observed.

Once Saleem exited the backseat, someone from the other car did the same. The two men walked up to each other, both with a bag in their hands. They spoke briefly, and just when they were about to do the handoff, Saleem looked back at the car while the bull tried looking to see who was inside. Our headlights were on, so they prevented him from seeing.

Moments later, the passenger door to the bull car opened, and before I could see who the person was, Saleem started to backpedal to the vehicle. Once Razor peeped the scenery, he placed the car in drive and inched up while I put my hand back to open the back door, giving him a head start to jump in.

By the time Saleem reached the car, the person's face had become visible... it was Naim.

"Go!" I shouted at Razor. "Drive, nigga!"

Saleem jumped into the backseat as Razor sped off before his door closed properly. A few shots were let off as we drove away, but only two connected on the back windshield. Luckily, it was a rental we were driving, and we used a fake ID to get it. The windshield was the least of my worries. I was just happy we got out of there fast as hell, and no one got hit.

"Fuck!" I growled, hitting the dashboard.

The following morning, I woke up from a light nap I took. After the incident happened, I went home but barely got any rest. I was so furious at how close it was we almost got caught up. While I want to say I didn't see it coming, I knew anything could have happened.

Quest wasn't home, and I knew he wanted to touch Naim himself, but it was getting harder and harder not to have the urge to off him myself. The nigga was outright disrespectful, bold, and retarded.

The only good thing about the situation was he couldn't have seen it was me in the whip. The rental was tinted out, it was dark, plus the headlights were on. The only way he would've known it was that Quest and I were attached to the transaction was because of Saleem. I could tell he was trying to set the bull up to buy the brick to see if it was his. For this exact reason, we repackaged all the bricks.

Ring. Ring.

My phone went off. Looking at the screen, I saw it was Razor.

"Yo," I answered.

"What we doin'?" he questioned.

"With what?"

"The stop."

"Open as usual but tell Saleem to fall back. I'll be at the crib," I informed him.

"Ard, say no more."

I decided it was best for me to stay home for the day to feel out the situation. Although Naim didn't see me, it was better to be safe than sorry. All it took was for a nigga to speculate, and they ran with shit.

Not trying to stress myself out, I relaxed and enjoyed a day inside. I texted a few of my lady friends to keep me occupied, including Naomi's fire ass.

> Me: You miss a nigga already or nah? 😏

> Naomi: Where is there to miss?

> Me: Everything. Let's not front.

> Naomi: If you're saying you miss me and want to see me, just say that.

> Me: I don't know about the missing part, but I won't mind seeing you.

> Naomi: Since you don't miss me, no!

> Me: I see you love to play games.

> Naomi: A whole lot. Let's see if you win the prize.

I just laughed at Naomi's text messages because she

was one of those flirtatious ass females who was hard to read. To me, Naomi looked like the type of jawn to talk heavy but don't give a nigga no play. That usually happened when they had a nigga in their life. Still, she wouldn't have entertained me if he were doing his job properly.

> Me: Keep playing with me, and you gon' see.

> Naomi: Well, I guess I'll see.

This girl. I shook my head.

The day went on as I kicked back in the crib. I ordered takeout while I laid back and watched movies and shit, something I barely got to do. The downtime was much appreciated, and it was needed.

While watching a movie on Tubi, my phone rang. It was one of my lil' jawns, Olivia, who I had coming over.

"You here?" I asked as soon as I picked up the phone.

"Hey, yeah, I'm outside," she informed me.

I paused the movie and went to the door. She was making it up the steps when I saw Tatianna and Khadijah getting out of a car and walking toward the house.

What the fuck? I thought. It was random as hell for Tatianna to bring her to my spot, especially without calling first.

"Hey, baby," Olivia sang as she wrapped her arms around my neck.

I gave her a quick hug and sent her inside. At that time, Tatianna and Dij were at the bottom of the steps.

"You ain't change one fuckin' bit. Bitches after bitches," Tatianna spouted.

"Bro, what the hell you talkin' 'bout. What y'all doing here?" I questioned.

It was Sunday, but I knew Khadijah wasn't coming over that weekend because she had to go away to play in a basketball tournament. I was expecting to see her the following Friday.

"So, your daughter needs a reason to come see her father?" she tried to switch it on me.

"Don't even do that, Tati. You had her away from me for years. Now, all of a sudden, you just want to pop up at my doorstep without calling first?"

"You know what? Fuck you, Khaleef," she spat. "Dij, let's go." She motioned for her to follow her. Before walking all the way off, Tatianna stopped and turned back around. "And fuck that court order. She ain't coming back here."

My baby and I didn't even get to greet each other properly since her mother and I started going at it from the gate. Dij walked away behind her mother with a sadistic face, which made me feel so bad.

It wasn't that I didn't want my daughter there. I just had to confront her mother about how she was moving. I was going to tell Olivia she had to go. That shit wasn't even anything to think or debate about, but Tati's hastiness to be confrontational made shit go left with the quickness.

I kept my cool because I knew every little thing could or would affect my case to get custody of Dij. That was my main focus in life — to get my daughter back with me, and I was going to make it happen by any means necessary.

NAOMI "NOMI" MOORE

"Girl, that episode had me dying laughing. They be drawn for real, for real," I exclaimed to Indigo.

We were on FaceTime talking about the show *Baddies* while I was at work. I was on the overnight shift that week, so I didn't have much to do during the nighttime.

"I'm sick of them." She laughed. "I'm just happy Philly's on there this season. Two of us at that."

"True. How are you feeling, though?" I inquired.

Indigo's morning sickness would come and go. One minute, she was able to eat properly, while the other, she couldn't keep anything down. My niece or nephew was tearing her up.

"I'm fine. I'm craving Taco Bell, though, which is

weird as hell." We both started laughing because that was just one place we didn't eat at.

"You better send a text to one of the guys and have them come bring it for you," I suggested.

After an incident happened with someone approaching her about Quest, I knew they had her at an Airbnb. Kha and his guys would pop in and out and carry her everywhere she had to go.

"Ehh, I'm thinking..."

As Indi continued talking, I received a text message from this girl I would cordially go out to the clubs with named Tasha.

> Tasha: I hate to be the one to do it...
>
> Tasha: Photo.

It was a picture of Naim and this same girl we had stopped dealing with each other over. They were all hugged up outside a lounge.

"I know this nigga's not serious," I blurted out.

"Wait, huh?" Indigo creased her forehead, all confused.

"This clown ass nigga is out with this bitch that I don't like, just embarrassing me," I summed it up quickly. "Fuck, I wish I had my car."

I had just gotten back my car from the accident I had, but then it had to go to another shop because the first set of people didn't do a proper job. Being without my own ride irritated my soul, especially for instances like this where I wanted to pull up on them.

"I mean, my car is here. I'll just shoot Kha a text and let him know I'm running out to meet you, so he knows I'm with someone," she offered.

"Indi, are you sure? It's one o'clock in the morning."

"Girl, shut up. I'm on my way," she insisted, then banged the phone on me.

That was one of the main reasons why Indigo and I were so close when we were in foster care. We had each other's backs no matter the situation, even if we knew it would result in us getting in trouble. That was my muthafuckin' girl for real.

While I started putting away the paperwork on my desk, I shot Tasha a text message.

> Me: They still there?

A few moments later, she texted back.

> Tasha: Nah, they just left.

> Me: Together?

> Tasha: Yeah, in Nai's car.

> Me: Ard, bet. Thanks, girl!

> Tasha: No problem. Make sure and beat that bitch's ass!

> Me: I definitely will be standing on business.

> Tasha: 💪💯

It wouldn't have been the first time I put my hands and feet on the bitch, Keisha. She was a pretty chocolate jawn. She had ass for days, something I didn't have, and a nice round C cup. Her stomach was flat, giving her that snatched look. She was one of those bold, thirsty ass hoes that had no respect for themselves, much less for anyone else. I let her slide the first time I caught them because she said Naim claimed he was single. The second time, I beat the dog shit out of her. And this time around would be the third time.

I finished putting away everything and straightened up my office. About twenty minutes later, Indigo called me and told me she was outside. Before I left, I gave my co-worker the heads up that an emergency came up. I also made sure to shoot my manager a text so that she'd see it the following morning.

Once inside the car, I told Indigo how to get to Naim's house. She didn't waste a second, pulling off from my job. Indigo's phone rang five minutes into the drive, and Kha's name popped up on the dashboard. We both looked at each other.

She clicked the answer button. "Yeah, bro."

"Where you at?" he got right to it.

"I just picked up Naomi from work. We're gonna grab some food and head inside," she half lied.

"This time of night?"

"Yeah, I'm hungry, and my friend needed me," she defended.

"Naomi could've called me to get her. I don't like the idea of you or her being out this late without any of us around, but ard, man."

My neck popped in Indigo's direction when Kha said that. We had been texting for a few days, ever since we both put together the surprise on Quest's behalf for Indigo. He was definitely growing on me, faster than a dude usually would, too.

"I'll call you when we get in," she assured him.

"Make sure you do."

"Ard." They hung up.

Indigo glanced at me with a wide smile. "Offering to pick you up if you needed him to?" she questioned with her brow raised and a devilish grin.

"Girl, it surprised me just as much as it surprised you." I smacked my lips.

"I guess my bro is feeling you or whatever."

"I guess so. I just might have to fuck around and see what he's about since my so-called dude is acting up."

I was so sick and tired of Naim's bullshit. Within the year we'd been together, it had been nonstop drama with him and women. If it wasn't him cheating, it was him not balancing his street life and his relationship right. A bitch was done being second to both matters.

We finally arrived at our destination. As she pulled up to his house, I saw his Charger parked outside, letting me know he was home. I was no fool. I knew Keisha was inside with him. Naim loved to be deep in some pussy after the club, which was the reason I always wanted to go out with him.

"Park right here," I instructed her as she pulled into an empty parking space about three houses down. "Stay here. I'll be right back." I got out of the car.

Walking up to the house, I walked around the side and made my way to the back. I used the spare key that Naim gave me in case of an emergency. In this case, it was deemed urgent for me to get inside. I climbed up the back steps and pushed the key inside the hole. So that I didn't make any noise, I slowly turned the key and the doorknob. Once inside, I quickly rushed over to the security system to see if I had to disarm it, but luckily for me, he didn't arm it back when he got inside.

Creeping through the kitchen, then the living room, I

tiptoed up the steps to the bedroom, where I heard moans. With every step, my heart felt like it was shredding into tiny pieces. When I reached the door, which was slightly ajar, my throat thickened with emotions at hearing the slapping noise of their bodies colliding.

Not able to take it anymore, I rushed into the room and saw Keisha on top of him with her feet planted on the bed, bouncing on his dick. When Naim saw me, his eyes turned big and round as saucers.

"Oh shit!" he blurted out and pushed Keisha off of him. When she turned around to see what startled him, she herself became shook. "Naomi," he started as he went to grab his boxers.

"Aht-aht." I lifted my hands up.

Not waiting another second, I dashed around the bed and grabbed Keisha's hair, but with one good tug, the wig came off. I flung the wig and started throwing punch after punch at her face and body. She had nothing on for me to grab, so I threw hands and feet wildly, making sure each one connected. She fought back, but my slim frame was too fast for her to keep up with.

"You nasty ass bitch."

Wap!

"Didn't I tell you to stay the fuck away from my man?"

Wap! Wap!

"Come here!" She tried to run.

I felt Naim wrap his arms around my waist and pull me away from her. "Nomi, chill!" He shouted.

Since he wanted to interrupt her ass whopping, it was his turn to feel my wrath as well. I kicked and swung at him after I elbowed him in the mouth. After a good amount of hits, he backed away, blocking his face, so that I had the opportunity to leap back across to Keisha's ass. She threw her hands up, ready to catch the fade, but once she swung and it didn't connect, I countered the punch, which landed right on her nose, breaking it instantly. Blood started to gush out rapidly.

Naim came back again, trying to separate us, so I started pouncing on him too. He must have had enough of me because he tried to grip me up, but I kept moving fast. Out of nowhere, I felt a hard blow to the side of my face, then another one on the side of my head. Naim literally balled his fist up and punched me like I was his equal. I stumbled back and saw him standing there, his chest repeatedly rising as he caught his breath.

"Did you really just hit me?" I asked in disbelief, holding my face.

"Yo, you in here drawn!" he barked.

Tears welled in my eyes as I felt totally betrayed. Not only did Naim fuck around on me with the same home wrecker, but he also put his hands on me for her.

At that moment, I knew what I had to do — leave. Not just leave his house but leave him alone entirely. It was time for me to move on and find someone who would treat me better. Naim was only going to be the downfall of me, and I couldn't let that happen.

I didn't utter a word. I just walked out of the room and made my way down the stairs. Naim didn't even run after me or anything. I wasn't sure if it was because I was hitting on him or if it was because he basically chose up. However, he didn't have to because I was done.

Rushing out of the house, I ran to the car and jumped inside. "Drive," I told Indigo.

She didn't ask any questions. She just pulled out of the parking space and peeled off Naim's block.

Tears were falling like it was a river as I started to break down and bawl. It started to hit me about what had happened and what I had been putting up with. I always loved to see the good and potential in people, but I had to learn when it just wasn't a good situation for me.

"Naomi, what happened?" Indigo questioned in a sincere tone.

I kept crying and couldn't get my words out, so she pulled over to console me. After a few moments in her embrace and listening to her soothing words, I started to calm down a little.

"Talk to me," she pressed.

I wiped my wet face with the back of my hand. "He hit me," I finally blurted out. "He chose that bitch over me. I'm done, Indi, I'm done!"

"He did what?" she screeched.

She jumped on her phone and called Kha. I saw his name pop up on the dash.

"What are you doing?" I asked, puzzled.

She lifted her finger up as he answered.

"Y'all cool?" Kha asked through the speakers.

"Some nigga put his hands on Naomi," Indigo informed him.

"What? Where y'all at?" his voice boomed throughout the car.

"I'm taking her to the Airbnb with me."

"I'll meet y'all there." He hung up.

"Why did you call him?" I quizzed.

"Because girl, that nigga, whoever the fuck he is, put his hands on you. I sure as hell can't do anything about it, but I know who could." She smacked her lips.

I'd never seen Indigo so enraged. It felt good to know I had people in my corner. Not caring to contest, I didn't say a word. For the remainder of the ride, I just sat back in my seat and stared out the window with a million things on my mind.

When we arrived at the Airbnb, Kha was already there. Instead of going inside, I told Indigo I wanted to go home. I appreciated her for taking me and being there, but I wanted to be alone to get my mind right. We said our goodbyes for the time being, and then Kha took me home.

The entire ride was quiet, with PNB Rock playing softly in the background. Kha hadn't asked me one question about what happened, which I appreciated since I was still trying to process everything. His presence alone made me feel calm and protected, though.

Pulling up to my house, Kha parked before I could just hop out. As I was sliding out of his Range Rover, he got out, too. Walking right behind me up the steps to my house, I saw him looking around. With the type of dude he was and into the streets, I wasn't surprised at how his head was constantly on a swivel.

"Thanks for bringing me home," I told him as I opened the door.

"That ain't nuffin'," he responded. I started to walk inside, but he gently grabbed me by the hand. "You gon' tell me what happened?"

Kha looked me straight into my eyes, and the vibe I got from him was sincere. I felt no reason to be defensive at that moment.

"Come on," I softly spoke, leading him into my house.

He closed and locked the door behind us. Kicking off our shoes, I headed toward the kitchen with him close behind. When I turned the light on and saw my face in the mirror, I jumped back in surprise.

The right side of my face was on fire, but once I saw the black and blue, it only confirmed how hard Naim had hit me.

"Fuck," I whispered.

Kha walked up behind me, then turned me around to take a look. "Where's this nigga at?" he calmly asked as he held my face with both his hands, rubbing his thumb across my bruised area.

I winced in pain. "I don't want you to get in trouble for me. It's fine," I tried to persuade him.

"Tell me this, and you can keep it real. There's no need to lie to me. Are you going back?" he questioned in a serious tone.

I shook my head with the quickness. "No. I'm done."

"Has he ever hit you before tonight?"

"No, it's the first time ever," I answered.

"And the last," Kha sternly added. "I don't believe in

abusing women. I have a daughter of my own, and I'd be damn if a nigga put their hands on her."

"I feel that."

"The only way I'ma put my hands on you is to choke yo' ass up when I'm deep in ya guts." He rested his hand around the back of my neck as he hovered over me and bit down on his bottom lip.

Kha was fine as ever, and he knew it. There was no denying our attraction to one another. Besides his looks, he had this way about him that made me want to be around him. I felt protected, and I felt lusted over.

"Maybe you need to put the right hands on me," I flirted. I covered my mouth quickly and giggled, making him chuckle as well.

"You sure you want that?" He eyed me intensely.

I nodded because I was unable to use my words. That man had me stuck and hypnotized.

With Kha's hand still at the back of my neck, he brought my head closer to his as our lips touched. Electric waves shot throughout my body as his tongue intertwined with mine. He caressed the back of my neck while his other hand roamed around my body, touching my breasts, hips, and ass.

In between kisses, we both helped undress one another until we were standing there naked as we were born. I looked down and saw he had a hook. Only once before had

I ever experienced a man with a hooked dick. That shit hit differently than a regular straight dick.

Moving from my neck to kissing and licking my breasts, Kha slipped his fingers inside of me, feeling how wet I was.

"Mmmm," I moaned out.

He slid his fingers out and turned me around so that I was leaning against the kitchen island. Bending down, he grabbed his sweats, pulled out his wallet, and grabbed a condom from it. Ripping it open, he slid the rubber down on his dick, then bent me over.

Kha gripped the shit out of my neck as he penetrated me with force. It was a burning pain, not because I wasn't wet, but because his size took my pussy by surprise. The pain quickly turned into pleasure by the fifth stroke. I was being pleased from the jump as he hit my spot every single time he thrust into me.

"Damn, this pussy is good," he whispered in my ear as he grabbed my hair and pulled me toward him.

My back was arched deeply, and I was throwing it back at Kha, matching his energy. The way he was fuckin' me, someone would've thought we'd been fuckin' for years. The chemistry and vibe were unmatched. The way Kha touched me while pounding my insides out sent me into a frenzy. He had the kind of dick and sex that'll make you go crazy, Left Eye crazy.

Sliding out of me, Kha picked me up, carried me over to the kitchen table, and laid me on it. He lifted both my legs straight up in the air as he slid right back inside of me. Grabbing onto my breasts, he used them to help him control the rhythm he was punishing my pussy with.

"Ohhh, fuck!" I cried out.

He opened my legs wide and wrapped his hand around my neck, giving it the right amount of squeeze. I felt myself flow down right on his dick when he did that.

"You like this shit?" he asked in a husky tone.

I started doing Kegels, making my hold on his dick even tighter than it already was. He stopped for a moment and closed his eyes. "Fuck," he whispered. I released, and then he started to make his way in and out of me again. I did it again, making him stop. Once I released, he slowly began to thrust in and out.

Speeding up his pace, I could tell Kha was about to cum. His hold around my neck became tighter, his strokes became deeper and harder, and he looked at me like he was ready to fuck me into the next week.

I felt myself cumming as he pressed down on my clit with his thumb. "You gon' come wit' me?" Kha asked in a seductive tone.

I nodded slightly since he had a hold on my neck.

Kha picked up his pace a little more again, and moments after, I felt myself peaking and my legs shaking.

As if on cue, he stopped deep inside of me, and I felt his dick pulsate.

"Shiiittt!" he groaned out loud.

He rested his head on my chest for a minute before standing back up and sliding out of me slowly.

I sat up on the table and just took him in. Kha was a work of art with tattoos all over his chest, arms, and neck. He had a six-pack that was very defined, and his dick looked like it was still hard, but it was actually soft. With such great sex, good looks, swag, and street mentality, I was ready to drop down on one knee and ask him to marry me.

"You tryna do again?" He stood there smirking.

I nodded and opened my legs for him.

We fucked like rabbits for the rest of the morning. The sun even met us up.

Indigo TAYLOR

"What? You got to be fuckin' lying." Quest bussed out laughing hysterically.

We were on our weekly visit, and I was filling him in on what had been happening outside the walls. I had to tell him about our late-night trip to Naomi's man's house.

"So, she went inside and fought both of them?" he asked in disbelief.

I nodded with a smirk on my face. "Yup, and she was in there for a minute, too. If I weren't pregnant, I would've gone inside. Plus, she told me to wait."

Naomi was a complete trip, and many of her ways hadn't changed since she was younger. She was always ready to pop off on whoever for whatever. Her hands were lethal, and she was calculated in how she fought. I used to tell her she needed to get into boxing or UFC fighting. That's how good she was. But she thought she was too pretty for a career path like that.

"Yo' ass better not have." He eyed me.

"Bae, come on. I ain't doing nothing to put me and the baby in harm's way," I reassured him.

"I know, baby. I'm just fuckin' with you." Quest leaned over and smirked, which made me blush.

That man had me all giddy inside. Things weren't perfect, but just being able to be around him made me feel complete.

"Oh, and Kha and Naomi are hunching, bae," I informed him.

"What? When the hell that started?" He backed up in shock.

"The same night she fought the bull and the jawn. He took her home, and well, I guess they had all the space and opportunity, and they took it." I laughed.

He covered his mouth while laughing. "Nah, niggas outta pocket. How you think that's gon' play out?"

"I have no clue. We just gon' have to wait and see. But this is all on you. You're the one who technically put them together."

If someone told me Kha and Naomi were going to start messing around, I would've told them they were lying. The first time they met was awkward. They both were sizing each other up on some territorial shit. Quest asking them to work together to surprise me was definitely when they connected and saw something in each other. I was all for it, especially because my friend deserved a solid person and not that dude she had, whoever he was.

"Me? Yeah, ard. All I wanted to do was make you feel special. Those two were just thirsty, baby," he joked.

"And you did make me feel special. Again, thank you so much for everything, my love."

"Ain't nuffin'. That's what I'm supposed to do." Quest leaned over, so I met him halfway to peck his lips.

"No kissing, no touching!" the supervising guard yelled at us.

We both looked at him and laughed.

"I wish I knew you planned to do all of that. I could've used that money to get my hearing aids," I mentioned.

His eyes widened, surprise and concern mingling. "Hearing aids? I didn't realize it was that bad already."

I shrugged, playing it cool. "Yeah, it snuck up on me faster than I thought, but it's ard."

"Indi," he called out, his voice low and serious in a way that made me meet his gaze. "I'll take care of it. You'll get your hearing aids and anything else you need or want. You have my word."

Quest's words wrapped around me like a warm blanket, easing some of the tension I'd been carrying. "You don't hav—"

"I said what I said, Indi. It will be taken care of."

Tears welled in my eyes as my emotions got the best of me. Quest just kept being my knight in shining armor, from the littlest to the biggest things.

"Thank you," I softly expressed.

"Anything for you, Chunks. I got you."

Silence came in between us as I thought about how lucky I was to meet him. God knew what he was doing with us. That's why I told myself I'd never question him.

Another visit had come and gone, and I was walking out of PICC without my other half. I turned my phone on to call Kha to let him know I was outside and ready to go. He came to the visit as usual, talked to Quest, and left us to be alone.

As I turned my phone on, I saw a message from my lawyer stating that I needed to contact him as soon as possible. Before I gave him a call, I called Kha, then stood in the shade away from the beaming sun to wait for him to pull up.

Eager to know what was up, I called Mr. Fairs.

"Thank you for calling Fairs and Associates. How can I help you?" the secretary greeted me.

"Hi, this is Indigo Taylor. Can I speak to Mr. Fairs, please?" I requested.

"Sure. He's expecting your call. One moment." She placed me on hold.

Within that time, Kha pulled up in front of the prison, so I swiftly moved to the truck and got inside.

"Hello, Ms. Taylor," Mr. Fairs jumped on the line moments later.

"Hi, I got your message when I got out of my visit. What's going on?"

"So, I spoke with your husband's lawyer. They would like to meet tomorrow to discuss some things. Are you up for it?"

I got quiet for a few seconds as I thought about it. *Did I want to really sit down with this man? Was it going to help the process move forward faster and smoother?*

"What do you recommend?"

"I say let's do it. So, this way, we know what he's looking for or where his head is," Mr. Fairs advised.

"Okay. Just let me know what time."

"I'll give the lawyer a call now, then I'll send you an email with the time and location."

"Okay. Thanks, Mr. Fairs."

"No problem. See you tomorrow."

Tomorrow it is.

I WOKE UP OPTIMISTIC ABOUT THE DAY AND HOW the meeting would go. We were to meet at my lawyer's office at ten o'clock that morning. The baby was acting right, so I wasn't feeling sick, which I was thankful for. I didn't want to be meeting with those people and feeling any kind of way. I might've just purposely thrown up on Malachi.

As usual, Kha came by and got me to take me to Fair's office. When we arrived, he stayed outside while I went in to handle my business.

When I walked in, the secretary immediately stood up. "Come with me. They're waiting for you," she informed me.

I followed her into the firm's conference room, where I saw all three gentlemen sitting around the table.

"Good morning, Ms. Taylor," Mr. Fairs greeted.

"Taylor?" Malachi started. "Her name is Anderson. And until then, address her as such."

His lawyer touched his arm, letting him know to simmer down.

"I understand your frustrations, but she is my client,

and I will address her as she prefers," Fairs shot back at him.

Period, I thought as I poked my lips out and raised my eyebrows.

"Anyway, shall we get started?" Fairs requested.

"Yes," answered his lawyer.

We began the meeting with verifying information, then got right down to the meat of things — the reason I wanted a divorce. I explained what I had experienced within the marriage, unhappiness, and then finding out about Malachi's affair and the baby on the way just put the icing on the cake.

The entire time I was talking, Malachi stared at me without blinking. He looked surprised at some of the things I spoke about, which were things I just kept to myself and never brought to his attention. He was probably wondering how I knew certain things. I had kept quiet for the sake of our marriage and trying to make things work, but that was all over now.

There was so much tension in the room that a knife would've had difficulty cutting through it.

"Do you want anything from the marriage?" his lawyer asked.

"No, I just want to be free of him," I simply stated.

Malachi dropped his head and chuckled.

"Since she doesn't want anything, why don't we make this process nice and easy?" Fairs suggested.

Malachi leaned over and whispered something in his lawyer's ear.

"From my understanding, your client is pregnant. Yes?" his lawyer inquired.

"Yes," Fairs truthfully answered.

"My client said the only way he will sign the divorce without a contest is when a paternity test is done. He believes the baby is his."

"Now you know damn well this baby ain't yours!" I snapped.

Mr. Fairs touched my arm and mouthed that I calm down. I sat back in my seat, fuming because I knew Malachi was all tricks and games. I couldn't for the life of me understand why he just didn't let me go.

"I know you're confident it's your boyfriend's, but let's just get it done once the baby is born, and it's over from there," Fairs whispered in my ears.

I thought about the length of time I'd have to wait to be legally unbound from Malachi. Then I thought about pushing out my child with Quest while still married to another man. While it didn't seem to go my way, it looked like I had no other choice.

I nodded at my lawyer.

"We will continue the process. I will draw up the

paperwork of the conditions, and when that time comes, and all is proven correct, in favor of my client, your client would sign, and they would go their separate ways."

"Sounds great," his lawyer spoke in a sarcastic tone.

"Are we done?" I questioned, with a hint of attitude.

"Yes, Ms. *Taylor*, I'll call you," Fairs told me, putting emphasis on the last name, Taylor.

Malachi shot him a menacing stare, then watched me as I got up and exited the office. I moved quickly, so I didn't have an encounter with him outside of our lawyers being present.

When I reached outside, Kha was on the phone but looking out the window. Once he saw me, he hopped out of the driver's side and waited for me to approach him. He started looking past me, so I turned around and saw Malachi exiting the firm and walking in my direction.

Kha opened the passenger side door. "Get in," he simply instructed.

While he walked back over to the driver's side, I saw him brandish his gun that was in his waistband. Malachi immediately stopped in his tracks. When Kha jumped in behind the wheel, he didn't waste any time pulling out of the parking spot and peeling off the block.

I thanked God Kha was around, but I was constantly praying for Quest to come home. I needed him.

QUESNEL Quest MACQUOID

I woke up to the same four walls again. Another day, the same routine in the Philadelphia Industrial Correctional Center. Every day felt like they just rolled it off a production line. I laid there, staring at the ceiling, thinking about Indigo. She was pregnant for the first time, and I wasn't there to experience it with her. Then, two different groups of people were after me and mine. Being inside didn't make things easier, either.

The CO came by my cell, banging on the bars. "MacQuoid!" he yelled. "Pack it up!" I thought maybe they were moving me out of solitary and back into the general population. It had been a while, and my mind was spinning with thoughts of what I'd faced there.

I got my stuff together, feeling something heavy in the

pit of my stomach. I felt in my gut that I would soon return to the hole shortly after I touched the cell block.

They didn't tell you much in here, so you learned to roll with whatever came next. I followed the CO down the long, dark corridors. The air smelled of metal and sweat. When he took me to processing instead of a unit, I thought maybe they were shipping me off to another facility. Maybe somewhere worse. My mind raced again. I then noticed they pushed my old clothes from before I got arrested across the counter.

It all became clear as day to me — I was going home. I held my sweats and Polo shirt in disbelief. It was what I'd been wearing the day they dragged me in here. It felt unreal that it was happening so soon. I thought I would've been waiting months for the appeal to go through.

After changing out of the prison clothes and into my own, the CO in processing made me sign some paperwork and then gave me instructions about going to see my PO. The moment I was finished, I was escorted outside of processing and out of the building altogether.

The sun hit me full force as I stepped outside, blinding and warm. It felt good to touch the outside concrete beneath my feet. When I looked to my left, I saw my lawyer, Cohen, standing there with a grin bigger than any I'd seen.

"Quest!" Cohen called out, rushing over. "Welcome

home again!" He pulled me in for an embrace and patted my back. "Your appeal was reviewed quickly, and well, you see the end result." He lifted his hands.

I couldn't believe it. I was free once again. Free to breathe fresh air, to move how a nigga wanted, and most of all, to see Indigo.

Cohen got serious for a minute. He asked me if I wanted to dig deeper into my original case and find out who set me up. I didn't have to think long. "Yeah, Cohen," I gave in. "Do whatever you have to. I need to know everything."

He nodded. "I'm on it."

We headed to his car as Cohen discussed plans and what we'd do next. I was thinking about Indigo, though, and about being there for her and the baby, making up for lost time. Although it was only about two months that I was inside, shit felt a little different now, like I'd been given a second chance.

The ride back into the city was calm. Buildings raced past the window, and people walked the streets. It was all so alive. I'd missed the noise and the chaos. It was funny how prison made you miss the things you thought you hated.

Cohen dropped me off at the tire shop before taking off. I peeped Kha's Range parked outside, so I knew he was there. I wasn't sure if he would've been at the shop since the whole shootout with Naim happened at the exchange.

When I walked onto the lot, some of the guys saw me, and a smile immediately came across their faces. I shot them all a head nod and continued inside. Behind the desk was Saleem, with his head down in his phone.

"This nigga's always watching Twitter porn," I joked.

His head popped up with the quickness, and once he saw who it was, he jumped to his feet and made it over to me. "The bull is out!" he shouted. We dapped one another up. The energy was definitely there so far. I felt loved. I felt missed.

"Kha's in the office," he informed me.

I wasted no time heading back to see my boy. When I walked in, I was blinded by what I saw. Kha was rocked back in his chair with his head back, getting head from what looked to be Naomi.

"Damn, this how I get welcomed home?" I blurted out.

Kha popped his eyes open, and they grew wider when he saw it was me. Naomi jumped and looked in complete shock as well.

"Quest!" he shouted.

"Man, get y'all shit together. I'm right outside," I told them, then left out the office laughing.

Not long after, they both came walking out of the office. As he was extending his hand for me to dap, I looked at it.

"You washed yo' hands, dickhead?" I raised a brow.

"Yeah, stupid. The fuck." We both laughed as we embraced one another.

"Hi, Quest," Naomi sang.

I looked at her with a smirk. "Mmm-hmm. What's good, Nomi?"

Everything Indigo told me about her just popped into my head, and I was laughing inside. It was cool that the two of them were having fun.

"Does Indigo know?" she asked.

I looked myself up and down. "Does it look like she knows?"

"Shut up." She rolled her eyes.

"She has a doctor's appointment today for two o'clock, bro," Kha informed me.

Kha, knowing Indigo's whole schedule, showed me he stood on business and did what I asked of him. He gave me his word that no harm would come her way and that he'd be there wherever she had to go. I believed him but seeing it for myself made him even more solid in my eyes.

"That's perfect. I need a cut, a good shower, and some new drip. Then I'll surprise her ass there," I responded.

"Say no more, let's go."

We dropped Naomi off at Airbnb to meet Indigo. Being right outside of where my lady was felt surreal. It took all of me not to jump out of the Range and run inside to her, but I wanted to get cleaned up first and surprise her in a meaningful place.

As soon as Naomi went inside, Kha headed to my apartment while he made a call to the barber for a house call. He offered him a payment that was nowhere near the average for a house call just to get him to come over as soon as possible. And by the time we reached my place, the barber pulled up a few minutes later, so I got my cut right away.

"Mmm-hmm, there he goes." I watched myself in the mirror after I finished getting my shit together.

I was feeling myself, and I knew Indigo's ass would've appreciated me looking clean rather than the woofed-out mess that I was on the inside and when I first met her.

"Go, pick her up, and take her to the doctor's like normal. Send me the address, and I'll take an Uber there," I instructed Kha.

I headed to the bedroom in search of my phone. Thankfully, it was inside my nightstand where Indigo said she put it so I could jump into action like I never left.

"Ard, that sounds like a solid plan," he agreed.

Kha gave me some money until he got to my stash to

return it to me. I also got my cards from the nightstand, so I was good to go.

Once he left, I jumped in the shower, staying in there for about an hour. I washed my skin from head to toe about seven times. I wanted to get the prison stench off of me. Once I was satisfied, I stepped out of the shower and dried my skin. I then headed into my closet and pulled out a calm fit — a Nike Tech sweatsuit and Jordans to match.

By the time I was finished getting dressed and situated, it was time to leave. I requested an Uber, which was only five minutes away at the time, so I grabbed my things and headed for the door.

Hopping into the backseat of the Uber, I peeped on the driver's GPS, and it said the ride would take about eighteen minutes. I took that time just to relax my brain for a moment and clear out all the bullshit so Indigo and my child could get the best of me. My mind went to how things would be when all the bullshit cleared up, and the baby was born. I thought about how I'd make them both happy.

With my mind on my family, the eighteen minutes

went by fast as well. We arrived at our destination, and I hopped out of the ride. I peeped Kha's Range, so I knew they were already there. I shot him a text because I didn't want to meet her in the waiting room. I wanted to walk in on the actual appointment.

> Me: Where's she at?

Seconds later, he texted back.

> Kha: She just went to get her vitals done before seeing the doctor.

> Kha: Come in.

I walked into the doctor's office, and all eyes shot my way. The women's eyes widened with lust as they took in my appearance. When my eyes landed on Kha and Naomi, they both smiled and got up.

"I spoke with the nurse already, so she's hip to what's going on," Naomi informed me.

"Good lookin'. Can we go in now?"

"Yeah."

Naomi led me to the nurse's desk, and then the nurse took us to the back. When I turned around, I saw Naomi recording on her phone. *Females man*, I thought. I didn't fuss about it because I knew Indigo would've eaten that shit up.

When we reached the door, the nurse opened it, and I saw Indigo getting up from her seat with her back turned to go onto the examination bed. Finally sitting down, she raised her head and immediately started crying.

Indigo TAYLOR

*T**his has to be a dream*, I thought to myself. I blinked, feeling as though my eyes were playing tricks. There stood Quest in the doorway, just staring at me. His appearance was slightly smaller than when he first went back into prison, but he was still my teddy bear.

I was speechless and felt as if I couldn't move a muscle in my body. Tears just flowed out of my eyes as I sat there motionless.

"Is that how you greet yo' man?" he asked with a grin that lit up the room.

I was so happy I couldn't stop the tears. They just spilled out like a river bursting its banks. My heart felt like it was singing.

"Quest!" I cried, jumping off the table to hug him tight. My arms wrapped around him, and I didn't want to let go. "You're home!"

We stood there, holding each other, and nothing else mattered. All the fear and worry from the last two months melted away. His presence was like a warm blanket on a cold night.

He pulled back slightly, looking deep into my eyes. "I'm here, Indigo, and I ain't going nowhere," he promised, and I believed him. Quest's words were like an anchor, steady and sure, keeping me grounded.

We kissed, his lips soft and familiar, and I knew I was finally home, too.

The doctor cleared her throat, reminding us there was still a little business to attend to. "Oh, sorry, sorry," I apologized as I climbed back onto the examination bed.

That was when I noticed Kha and Naomi were in the room as well. While they stayed to the side and out of the way, Quest came and stayed by my side, holding my hand.

The room dimmed as the doctor turned on the ultrasound machine. I lifted my shirt as she spread the cool gel on my belly, and the screen soon flickered to life. We watched in awe as the grainy images appeared. But then, something unexpected happened.

The doctor tilted her head, eyes focusing on the screen.

"Well, this is a surprise," she said, her voice tinged with amazement. "It looks like there isn't a baby in there."

"Huh?" both Quest and I spoke in unison.

"Yup, I stand correct. There isn't a baby in there. There are actually three babies in there," she excitedly disclosed.

My jaw dropped, and I glanced at Quest, who was just as stunned. "Triplets?" he whispered with his eyes wide in disbelief.

I looked over at Kha and Naomi, who both were in complete shock.

"Three," the doctor confirmed, pointing to the little blobs on the screen. "See? Three strong heartbeats."

My heart soared, filling with joy, excitement, and a dash of panic. *What in the hell was I going to do with three babies when I never even had one before?*

Quest squeezed my hand, and I felt his excitement radiate through me. "Everything is gon' be ard, Chunks," he assured me. He must have noticed the mixed emotions I had.

We listened as the doctor played the heartbeats, each a tiny drumbeat of life. It was the sweetest music I'd ever heard. The rhythm of our future, promising love and laughter, and all the adventures to come. Something I dreamed of having for years. I couldn't believe I would finally have happiness like I had always wanted since I was a young girl.

I looked at Quest, and our eyes met in shared wonder. "This can't be real," I softly uttered, tears of joy springing to my eyes again. My hands trembled a bit as I reached up to wipe them away.

Quest nodded, brushing a stray tear from my cheek. "It's real, baby girl, and only God made this shit happen," he stated, his voice full of emotion.

We sat there, surrounded by the steady beat of our babies' hearts and our loved ones. And in that moment, everything felt perfect. Life had thrown us a curveball, but we were ready to catch it with open arms.

AFTER WE LEFT THE DOCTOR'S OFFICE, QUEST, Kha, Naomi, and I went out to eat at Ruth's Chris Steakhouse on Market Street. I loved their food, and Quest deserved to eat properly after being damn near starved in solitary confinement. My man shed some pounds but still had that big build, so I knew I would have to live in the kitchen to get him back right.

Once dinner was over, Kha drove Quest and me back

to the Airbnb, while he and Naomi went about their way. As soon as we walked into the house, Quest didn't wait a second before he was all over my body.

He wrapped his arms around me from behind and planted kisses on my neck while we walked to the bedroom. Turning me around, he grabbed my face with both of his hands and kissed me gently. Once our tongues intertwined, the passion intensified, and the kissing sped up.

"I missed yo' ass," Quest whispered in between kisses.

"I missed you more, baby," I softly expressed.

We started to peel off our clothes one by one until we were fully naked. I touched his smooth skin and admired the tattoos all over his body as if it were my first time seeing them.

Quest laid me down on the bed and spread apart my legs. As he brought his face to my lady part, my breathing picked up in anticipation of the feeling. He blew on my clit, then licked it in a circular motion. I caressed his head as he latched onto my clit and sucked it.

"Oh, baby," I moaned out in pleasure.

Not being touched in two months was driving me insane. I was feeling hornier than usual, and my panties were always soaked.

Quest flicked his tongue all around my pussy, then made his way to my ass hole. I jumped at the initial contact but settled once I enjoyed the feeling. Moving my hips in a circle, he pressed down on my knob with his tongue as he slid two fingers inside of me.

"Damn, Chunks, you wet as fuck," he blurted out.

I looked down between my legs and just saw his head moving about my happy place. My belly was in the way of seeing the full view, but I didn't give two fucks. The feeling was everything.

Giving my pussy one long lick, he slid his dick into me in one swift motion.

"Quest," I softly asserted, out of breath.

He placed both his hands on either side of my face while he had my legs up in the air, pounding his way in and out of me. The way he stared deep into my eyes while delivering long, sweet, deep strokes, I knew he was trying to make sure he was the only man I ever wanted. Physically, Quest had me gone. Mentally, he had me wide open.

With every stroke, I felt myself dripping more and more. I watched the muscles in Quest's arms tighten as he gripped my waist, giving him the right hold to bring my body to his. The pleasure that was written all over his face told me my pussy was doing what it needed to do, and his dick and sex game always understood the assignment.

Quest turned me over gently but kept me on all fours, so I wasn't on my stomach. Sliding right back in me, he grabbed my hair with one hand, then pressed my back in, making me arch my back with the next. Starting slowly, he gently hit my spot and would stay for a second before pulling out and going back in. After a few moments, he sped up as I threw my ass back. All that could've been heard in the room was our skin slapping and my pussy sounding like cheesy macaroni.

The way Quest was fuckin' me, I swore he was trying to get me pregnant on top of this pregnancy. While the physical touch was everything, mentally, we both were missing each other, so the sex was top of the line.

We went at it for a while before Quest finally came. Still, we weren't one and done. Even with my pussy sore, our lovemaking went on for hours. I was on cloud nine, and I knew he was, too.

QUESNEL "Quest" MACQUOID

With the way Indigo's pussy was feeling, I didn't want to come up out of it. I could've stayed in that shit for days at a time. I knew I was tearing her thick ass up, so I let her rest. Plus, I ain't want to be having my babies moving all about inside of her. Just the thought of having three children sent chills down my spine.

I looked over at a sleeping Indigo and saw how peaceful she looked. That's all I wanted to do — bring peace into her life. She deserved it, and so did I. Most of all, our children deserved happy and healed parents.

My phone vibrated, and I knew it could only be one person — Kha. When I grabbed it from the nightstand, I saw it was indeed him.

"Yo," I answered.

"I'm outside. Let me in."

Oh shit, I cursed myself. I forgot I told him to come and check me. It was a good thing Indi was fast asleep, or else I wouldn't have heard the end of it. Kha and I had pressing matters to discuss, though.

I quietly slipped out of bed and threw on some basketball shorts. I then made my way out of the room, making sure to close the door softly behind me. When I got downstairs and opened the front door, Kha was already there, waiting.

"Wassup, bro?" Kha dapped me up, then walked inside.

He took off his sneakers and went into the living room to get comfortable.

"Shit, you tell me. Fuck goin' on?"

"That goofy ass nigga Naim gotta go, my nigga. ASAP, too," he sternly spoke.

I was caught up on all the mess that nigga had been doing. Besides the run-ins with my team, other people had his name in their mouths, and it wasn't a pleasant taste. He was terrorizing the city. Naim was always a hothead and a ruthless nigga, but he never did shit out of spite or just because. In the past, he had always had a plan and moved properly. I guess fucking around with Big Ak had him moving wild and sloppy.

"No cap. Ain't no way around that," I agreed. "He's a wild bull. That nigga played a part in me getting put away. Then he had the nerve to pull up on my shorty and touch her? And he wanna buss shots at y'all? Yeah, he's a fool... a dead one, too."

"We gotta hit him before he hit us. Ye mean?"

"Most definitely. We gotta get the drop on him."

"I was only waiting for you to tell me what to do. I'll find a way and keep you posted. He gotta lie down like yesterday."

I nodded in agreement. "Keep me posted, bro."

We both stood and dapped each other up. He made his way to the door to put his sneakers on.

"You pulling up to the shop tomorrow? Ol' head's gon' be calling," he informed me, referring to his pops, Khaleef Sr.

"Yeah, I'll be there after I make a few moves in the morning."

"Ard, bet."

When Kha headed out, I went into the kitchen and heated up my leftovers. Once I was finished, I went back upstairs to slide back into Indigo.

The following morning, I woke up to pussy and breakfast in bed. We literally fucked about twenty times from the night before and throughout the morning. I was tired as hell, so I knew Indi was, but she still got up and made us breakfast.

After we fucked up the food, we got ourselves showered and situated to start our day. She had work, and I had to go and see my new PO before heading to the shop. I just prayed it was no dickhead like Anderson that time around. I didn't have the energy to deal with someone like that again. Besides having to see my new PO, I did want to inquire about what happened to Anderson since they saw he wrongfully violated me.

"Let's go, Chunks! Yo' ass gon' be late!" I yelled upstairs.

Indigo had to be at work at eight a.m., and the time was already seven thirty. I didn't have any set time to go to the probation office, and of course, Kha didn't clock me when it came to arriving to work at the shop. Leave it up to him, and I didn't have to show up at all.

"I'm coming now!" she hollered back.

A few moments later, she made her way down the steps to me. I took in her appearance and couldn't deny her beauty and elegance.

"You look gorgeous, baby," I complimented her.

She blushed. "Thank you, my love." We pecked each other on the lips.

Putting on our shoes and sneakers, we finally walked out of the door and made our way to her car. I opened the passenger side door for her to get in, then rounded the vehicle to the driver's side. I was going to hold the car for the day, so I had to drop her off to work before I made my move.

Starting up the car, I pulled off and headed toward her job on Broad Street. It was thirty minutes with morning traffic. We held hands and listened to music the entire ride.

When we arrived at her job, she didn't even want to get out of the car. I had to literally drag her ass out of the car to go inside. I gave her a nice wet kiss and slapped that phat ass as she walked away.

"Have a good day, Chunks." I winked.

"You too, Big Boy." She blew me a kiss.

Big Boy? I like that shit.

I hopped back behind the wheel and took off toward the probation office. It was a quick fifteen-minute drive down Broad Street. Before I knew it, I returned to the very place I dreaded.

Parking up the car, I got out, locked it, and headed inside. Remembering the process well, I went through security and signed in. Since I wasn't sure who my new probation officer was, I made sure to let the person at the desk know that it was a first-time check-in with them.

I sat and waited for about twenty minutes before my name was finally called. It was a short Spanish woman standing there waiting for me. I approached her as she looked me up and down.

"MacQuoid?" she asked.

"Yeah."

She motioned for me to follow her. I thought she was a secretary or something until we walked into an office, and she took a seat behind the desk.

"You're my new PO?" I quizzed.

"I am. My name is Samia Sanchez. You will address me as Ms. Sanchez or just Sanchez."

She seemed cool, but still not someone I'd trust. The first impression showed me she was not an Anderson, but who was I to say? It was only the first meeting.

I nodded. "Sounds good."

She started looking in my file for a moment but kept glancing at me. "I will keep this short and simple. I read over your file, and although everything has been verified, I need to verify it myself, especially after what happened with your case," she explained.

I nodded and continued to listen.

"I'll come by the workplace you have listed, as well as your residence."

"Do I need permission to move?" I inquired.

After everything that had gone down, Anderson and Naim knew where I laid my head, which was a no-go. It was imperative that Indigo and I moved to a new spot, so I decided we'd occupy the Airbnb until we found somewhere more permanent.

"Yes, and no. What's the problem? Are you trying to move?" She raised a brow.

"I'm currently staying at an Airbnb until my lady and I find a new place. It just isn't a comfortable situation there," I briefly explained.

"Your lady, huh?" She tilted her head and smirked.

I don't know if I was trippin' or was she low-key flirting with a nigga.

"Yeah," I simply answered.

"I'll need the address of the Airbnb and as soon as you find a new place, please make sure to get that address to me as well."

"Ard, no problem. I have a question."

"Wassup?"

"What happened with my last PO?" I finally came out and asked.

Sanchez dropped her head and chuckled a bit. "Anderson has been fired following the incident with you. I can't go into further detail on the matter, but he's no longer here," she revealed.

Wow, they actually held him accountable.

"Oh, ard."

"Just please let me know if he ever tries to contact you or anything like that. Anderson has strict orders to stay away."

"Ard. Are we good here?"

"Just confirm all your information on this form, sign it, and you're good to go unless you have a reason to stay." She lightly blushed, but I caught on.

Yeah, she's definitely flirting with a nigga.

I read through the form with all my personal information on it. Once I saw everything lined up correctly, I signed and stood to my feet.

"Have a good one. See you next week," Sanchez stated as I walked out.

"Mmm-hmm. Stay out of trouble!" she yelled over my shoulder.

I left out of there confused as to what the hell type of time she was on. Sanchez was definitely easy on the eyes, but she ain't have shit I wanted. My heart was taken. Indi was all a nigga needed.

After I left from seeing my new PO, I went straight to the tire shop to see what they had going on there. I wasn't dressed to work, but I had planned on sticking around, especially because my ol' head was scheduled to have a video visit with Kha.

"Ayooo, I just got into my old Facebook account," I blurted out.

I was laid back on the couch in Kha's office while we were in our own worlds on our phones. While waiting for ol' head to call, I was scrolling through my phone and decided to try to get into my old social media accounts. Luckily, I still had access to my email address for the Facebook account, so I got in.

"Fuck you need to be on Facebook for, dickhead?" Kha joked. "Ain't nuffin' but trouble on that bitch."

"I could only imagine," I agreed.

My Facebook was old as hell, so I knew it had a lot of family and old associates on it. I wasn't tryna reconnect with no one. The thing I wanted to do most was go into the photos and save them for memories. When I went into them, I saw a bunch of pictures of Kaedon from when he was a newborn baby until his late age.

Seeing his handsome little face took me back to the days we had together. I spoiled the shit out of Kaedon. That little boy had the latest designers, games, you name it. Besides me giving him everything he wanted, he deserved it. He was well-mannered and respectful, and at only four years old, he loved to help around the house.

As I clicked on picture after picture, it hit me that his birthday was approaching in another week. Since I had been home, I didn't get to visit his or my mother's grave. I didn't even know where they laid them to rest.

I went and searched Cohen's number and pressed the call button.

"Yeah, Quest. Is everything alright?" he answered on the second ring.

"Yeah, everything is cool. Listen, I need a favor."

"Anything. How can I help?"

"I need to locate my son and mother's graves. You could do that?" I inquired.

"Definitely. Send me the correct spelling of their names, their birthdays, and the day they passed."

"Ard, say no more. I'm about to text you it now."

"Cool. I'll get back to you with the information," he assured me before hanging up.

Although I knew it would be hard, it was time I went and visited them.

"Oh, there he goes," Kha announced as the video call was coming through.

I jumped up and went over to where Kha was. As soon as ol' head appeared on the screen and saw us, he had a wide-ass smile on his face.

"Asalaam Walaikum, my young'ns!" he greeted.

"Walaikum Asalaam," Kha and I responded in a unison.

Although I wasn't Muslim, if one greeted me, the respectful thing was to greet them back.

We all chopped it up for the thirty minutes he had on the call. It was great seeing and hearing from him. Without him, I didn't know how far I would've gotten when I first touched back home. Linking me with his son was the perfect move, and my agreeing to it was the best decision I made. Those two men were my family, the only family I had besides Indigo and the babies. I loved them real bad and would do anything for any of them... even kill.

Indigo Taylor

After spending a crazy night with my man, I was not ready to leave his side. During the entire shift at work, I texted him like an obsessed stalker.

> Me: Tell me how much you miss me...

Big Boy: I miss you more than I miss these streets, and you know a nigga love these streets.

> Me: 😘

Me: I'm missing you somethin' crazy. My pussy is hurting, but I want you inside me.

> Big Boy: You sure you want more? Because I ain't gon' take it easy.

> Me: Ain't like I'ma run.

> Big Boy: Run on this dick. 🍆

Just as I was about to respond, a patient approached the desk.

"Hi, I was told to bring this back to the front desk for Dr. Hero. She said you would bring it up to her," she mentioned.

Dr. Hero did give me a heads-up that a patient was going to come back with an envelope, and I was instructed to bring it straight to her.

"Sure, I'll take it to her," I informed her.

I slipped my phone into my cardigan pocket as she walked off before heading for the elevator. When I reached the fifth floor, I got off and made my way to Dr. Hero's office. Knocking on the door, she opened it right away.

"Here's the package you wanted." I handed the envelope over to her.

"Thank you so much, Indigo."

"No problem." I smiled and turned to leave.

As I walked back toward the elevator, a woman was standing there waiting for it. She looked to be around my age and was dripped out in designer. She turned my way for a split second, and I saw it looked like she was crying or at least getting ready to.

Ding.

The elevator reached our floor, and we both got on. As soon as the doors closed, she broke down, crying hysterically. When she held onto her stomach, I noticed she was pregnant. Immediately, I felt the need to console her since I, too, was pregnant and knew the emotional roller coaster she was experiencing.

"Hey, love, it's okay." I came closer to her so she could see my face.

She wiped away the tears from her bloodshot red eyes. "It would never be okay," she cried.

Ding.

The elevator reached the first floor. I helped her off, and we sat down on the bench in the hall near the front desk.

"What's going on? Is everything okay?" I questioned, trying to see if I could help solve the problem or at least be of any assistance.

She sniffled. "I miss my son so much," she expressed.

"Where is he?" I pried, but only to get a better understanding of her pain.

"He's dead. He's dead and never coming back."

I couldn't even start to imagine what she was going

through. Immediately, Quest came to mind because he had to endure the same hurt and pain.

"I know you may not want to hear it, but he's in a better place now."

"It's no better place than being with his mother. I just want my baby back," she continued.

I rubbed her back and rocked her gently.

"His birthday is coming up, too, and he's not here to celebrate."

"Shhh, shhh. It's going to be okay," I encouraged.

For a while, we talked until she calmed down and stopped crying. Once she was okay enough to leave, I walked her to the front of the building, where she jumped into an Uber.

When I returned to my desk, I pulled out my phone and saw I only had half an hour left of work. Just when I was about to shoot Quest a text to let him know he better be on time to get me, a call came in from Naomi.

"Hey, girl," I answered.

"You still at work?" she quizzed.

"Yeah, why?"

"I'm around the area. You drove?" she questioned.

"Nah, Quest dropped me off. I was just about to tell him to be on his way."

"Don't bother. Text him and tell him I'll get you," she offered.

"You sure, Nomi?"

"Girl, shut up. I'll be there in a few minutes," she told me before hanging up.

I quickly shot Quest a text, letting him know Naomi was going to pick me up and I'd see him back at the house.

The countdown to clock out came around fast, and in no time, I was then walking out of the building and into Naomi's car.

"You finally got your shit back, huh?" I teased her as I sat in the passenger seat.

Naomi had been going back and forth with mechanics, straighteners, and her insurance company for a while. I was happy she was finally back, pushing her own whip.

"Girl, real funny." She watched me out of the corner of her eye.

"What? I'm telling the truth. This shit was gone way before we even reconnected."

"Alright, that's enough. I—"

Her phone started ringing, cutting her off.

"What do you want?" she answered, then listened to whoever was on the other end of the phone. "Listen, I already told you what it was. I'm done. Go ahead and put yo hands on the next bitch."

Judging by her conversation, I knew it was her old dude on the phone.

"Where you at? Because I'm coming for my keys. I

don't need you being weird." She listened to the person again. "Cool, I'm coming now," she last said, then hung up. "Indi, I need to make a quick stop to get my keys from that nigga. Is that cool?" she asked.

"Yeah, boo. Go ahead."

I checked my phone to see if Quest had texted me back, but he didn't, so I figured he had gotten busy.

Naomi maneuvered through the Philly streets to wherever her destination was. We drove for about twenty minutes, and all I heard was her complain about the dude. It was crazy to me that I never learned his name or knew how he even looked. Not that it mattered anymore because she was done with him and had Kha's nose all up her ass.

She bent the corner off of Broad Street near Temple University. Driving down a few blocks, she turned right onto a street and pulled up behind a Charger. Looking around, I noticed it was the same place I drove her to when she went inside and started sharing ass whoppings.

"Hold on," she told me and jumped out of the car.

I watched her walk up to the Charger and knock on the window. Seconds later, the door opened, and a guy exited the car. When I was looking to see how he looked, a text came through from Quest, grabbing my attention.

> Big Boy: I'm at the shop. I'll be here for a minute. Let me know when you get inside.

> Me: Okay, baby.

I locked my phone and returned my attention to Naomi and her drama-filled life outside. She had her hands all in his face. I had prayed he didn't swing on her again because I couldn't sit in the car and let that happen, pregnant or not.

He handed her something, which I assumed were her keys, and then she stormed back to the car. Not wasting another second, she put the car in drive and pulled off. As she passed him, still standing outside his car, I caught a perfect view of his face. When I realized who it was, my heart dropped into my ass. It was the bull, Naim.

"Naomi! What's his name?" I raised my voice loud.

I started to get furious.

"Naim, why?" she looked clueless.

"Naomi, do you know who the fuck that is?"

"What you mean, Indigo? That's my now ex-boyfriend. You know him?" she quizzed.

"That's Quest's old best friend, the one he's beefing with right now," I revealed.

She pulled the car over abruptly. "What?"

"Yes!"

"That's the bull you was telling me pulled up on you and threatened y'all?" Her eyes grew wide.

"Yes!"

"Fuckkk!" She started punching the steering wheel.

"Listen, I love you, but Quest and Kha have gotta know this shit," I chided. "It's either you gon' tell 'em, or I will."

Silence filled the car for a few moments.

"Okay, I will," she finally stated.

"They're at the shop. Let's go."

Naomi placed the car back in drive and pulled away from the curb and onto the street. The closer we got to the tire shop, the worse my nerves became. My anxiety was shooting through the roof with the information that I knew.

I wasn't sure how the guys were going to react, but Naomi had no other choice but to tell them. Once she told them the truth about not knowing about Naim and their beef, I believe they would be understanding. One thing I knew for sure, though, was that she would have to pick a side for real and show her loyalty card.

We finally arrived at the tire shop. As I got out of the car, I saw Naomi being hesitant to get out. When I turned around and shot her a look, she quickly slipped out and locked the door. I walked onto the lot and made my way inside the office, where I saw Razor behind the desk.

"Indi! Wassup!" he greeted me.

"Hey, Razor, where are they?" I questioned.

He pointed to the back. "In the office."

"Thanks." I turned around and motioned for Naomi to follow me.

As I got outside the door, I could hear the guys inside talking and laughing. The mood was going to quickly change once she told them everything she needed to tell them.

Knock. Knock.

I waited for them to grant me entry.

"Come in," I heard Kha state.

I pushed the door open and saw Quest on the couch, Kha behind his desk, and Saleem on the chair with his foot on the desk. When they saw us, they all smiled.

"Wassup, Chunks?" Quest asked.

I turned to Naomi. "Talk! Tell them and don't leave shit out," I demanded.

The guy's smiles quickly turned into frowns as they braced themselves for what was coming next.

QUESNEL *Quest* MACQUOID

"What the fuck did she just say?" Kha questioned, creasing his forehead in confusion.

There we were, stuck and trying to process what the fuck Naomi just told us. I knew it had to be something serious, especially with the way Indigo barged in and demanded she speak. Never in a thousand years would I have thought it was going to be her telling us her ex, who she recently broke up with, was none other than Naim.

"Naomi, I'm going to ask you this one time, and one time only. Did you know Naim was beefing with us?" I sternly asked.

"No, I had no idea. If I did, why would I have taken

Indigo with me today to get my keys from him?" she pointed out.

Although we were on edge at that point, she did make sense of what she was saying. It would've been a dead giveaway to take Indigo around him, knowing what was going on. I believed her.

"Who side are you really on, though?" Kha spoke up and asked.

"What do you mean?"

He stood up from his seat behind his desk. "Exactly what I just asked. Are you fuckin' with him or with us? This ain't a game, Naomi."

"I don't fuck with him anymore."

"But would you be okay with seeing the nigga dead?" Kha pushed.

Naomi looked shook as she watched all of us in the room. "If it means all y'all, especially Indigo, are protected, then yes," she answered.

Kha shot me a look, then sat down.

"Another thing, Naomi," I added.

"What?"

"I need a drop on his location. This will show us if you're really with us or just straddling the fence because you're in our presence."

"I'm telling you, I'm with y'all. What the fuck?"

"So, about that location."

Indigo started to speak, but I lifted my finger to silence her.

"I will give it. It's not a problem. Just please don't let that shit backfire on me," she pleaded.

I looked over at Kha, who was staring at the wall.

"Y'all go outside for a minute," I told the girls.

They both left out of the room without saying another word.

"What you thinkin'?" I inquired.

"I'm ready to go the moment she drops that location. I ain't tryna bullshit around. It's a reason this information just dropped in our laps," Kha voiced.

"Yeah, I feel you. And if we sit on it, and he finds out she's fuckin' with you, it's only going to make it harder to get to him. That muthafucker is like a ghost right now. No one knows where he lives, and he's right here in the fuckin' city."

"Naomi ain't even gotta do nothing. Let's get the addy, post up, then light his ass up when he least expects it," Saleem chimed in.

I looked at Kha and shrugged. He lifted his hands in the air, indicating it was whatever.

"Indigo!" I shouted for her to hear through the door.

Moments later, she walked in with a blank expression. "Yeah?"

"Tell Naomi to come here," I instructed.

She walked in slowly. "Wassup?"

"What's the address?" I came straight out and asked.

Not hesitating, she read out the address with the quickness. I called Razor into the office and gave him strict instructions to take the girls to the Airbnb and stay with them. Indigo didn't want to leave me, but I had to talk her down and let her know this was the side of me I didn't want her to witness.

I rubbed her stomach, talked to the triplets, and gave her some kisses before I sent her on her way. Kha didn't say a word to Naomi, and I knew she felt a way. I couldn't tell the nigga how to feel, especially with him just learning everything. When the dust cleared, I told myself I'd holla at him when the time was right.

We loaded our guns and got ready to make a move. There was no telling if Naim would've been home or not. Either way, we were pulling up on his block. Kha called his man, who had scrap cars meant for situations like this. Once we got the green light for one, we left the shop and drove to his garage, which was not far from where we were.

After we switched out the cars, Kha, Saleem, and I drove to the address Naomi gave us. On the ride there in the backseat, I just kept thinking to myself, how did we get to that point... the point of wanting to kill each other instead of killing for each other? Naim had crossed a lot of lines, and even if I wanted to forgive him for some shit, he had done so many other things that made his grave deeper. There was no coming back from this. My mind was made up.

"This the block right here," Saleem stated as he drove down it.

All three of us were looking at the numbers on the houses and checking to see if his car was parked outside. As we reached halfway down the street, I peeped a black Dodge Charger.

"Ain't that Naim's car right there?" I pointed it out to them.

"Hell yeah, it is," Kha confirmed.

Saleem pulled into an open parking space, cutting the engine and lights.

We sat back as we observed our surroundings. It was near Temple University up in North Philly. It looked like the usual Philly urban block. It was nothing fancy, but neither was it rundown. Naim had taken a page out of my book not to put yourself out there, no matter how much money you made — blend in.

The time was 7:42 in the evening. The sun had recently set, and the night sky was slowly taking over. The block was quiet already, with barely anyone moving about, which was a good thing in our case. There was no one to see an unfamiliar car sitting around with three niggas inside. Granted, the car tints were black, but if someone was like me with excellent vision, they would've made us out.

We didn't have a plan on how to get in his crib, so we decided to wait it out for him to come outside. It was still early, and if Naim was anything like he used to be, he was going to leave out the house before the night was over.

THREE AND A HALF HOURS HAD PASSED, AND there was still no sign of Naim. I was starting to think Naomi tipped him off or something. However, when I saw his door open and he walked out, I cursed myself for thinking like that toward her. I knew the situation was sticky, but she has shown her loyalty to us so far.

"Look that dickhead right there," Saleem pointed out. "Let's light him up right fuckin' now."

"Hold on, hold on," I tapped his shoulder as I looked through the windshield at him.

He was on the phone, running his mouth, oblivious to his surroundings. It seemed like the perfect time to drive up and spray his ass, but first, I had to make sure there was no one outside or lurking.

Naim was still standing on his front steps on the phone. I looked around and saw the coast was clear, so I gave Saleem the green light to pull up.

He started the car, which caught Naim's attention. Once Saleem saw Naim look in our direction, he instantly placed the car in drive and pulled off, speeding toward him. Kha and I rolled down our windows and aimed straight at him. Naim dropped his phone, pulled his gun from his waist, and started letting shots off back our way.

From where we were, I saw his white t-shirt under his sweater filled with red spots, letting me know we caught him. I emptied my clip in his ass, and I know Kha did as well, judging from the amount of shots I heard.

Naim dropped onto the ground at the bottom of the steps, face down. Once I peeped that he wasn't moving, I told Saleem to drive off.

"That's what the fuck I'm talkin' 'bout, dickhead!" Saleem shouted as he drove.

"This nigga's the bid." Kha laughed, referring to Saleem and his antics.

I quietly sat in the backseat with nothing to say. My mind raced with memories of Naim and me growing up being Batman and Robin. That was my dawg. I never saw the day we'd been on opposite sides of each other's guns. While the shit hurt me to do, I had to put myself and my family first. It was kill or get killed. It was me or him.

One Week Later...

After taking out Naim, we kept our ears glued to the streets to find out if he indeed died or survived the hit. There weren't any immediate news articles or coverage of his death, so for a moment, we thought he was still alive. Then, the R.I.P. posts started to circulate on social media, confirming his death.

"Baby, are you okay?" Indigo asked.

I woke up feeling heaviness in my heart. It was Kaedon's birthday. He would've been fourteen years old. I thought about how his life was going to be at that age and started feeling emotional as fuck.

"I'll be ard. Thanks," I simply told her.

"Did Cohen ever call you back with the plot information?"

Two days before, Cohen had shot me a text with Kaedon's and my mother's grave information. I was happy he got it to me just in time for his birthday so I could visit him.

"Yeah. I got his and my moms," I informed her.

"Well, let's go before time consumes us," she suggested.

Indigo planned to go with me to visit Kaedon from the moment she found out that was what I wanted to do. She was very supportive and patient with me, which I appreciated.

"Ard, let's go." I agreed.

We left out of the house and found a flower shop to grab some things to put on Kaedon's grave, such as balloons, flowers, candles, and toys. Once we got everything we needed and wanted, we made our way over to William Pen Cemetery.

The weather was beautiful, with the sun shining brightly on the June afternoon. No rain clouds were in sight, giving us a promising time with Kaedon. When we arrived at the cemetery, we parked and grabbed the things out of the car. Looking for the plot number Cohen given me, we finally landed our eyes on it.

"Look, bae." She pointed. "His stone is beautiful."

I walked in front of his headstone and couldn't believe I was reading, "Rest in Peace, Kaedon

MacQuoid." I asked myself why it couldn't have been me instead.

While I stood there in a daze, Indigo decorated his headstone and grave. I looked on as she made it look nice and lively.

"You like it?" she asked me with a big smile, referring to how his grave looked when she was finished.

I nodded. "Yeah, I love it."

She stood back on her feet and came next to me. Holding my hands, she leaned her head on my shoulder.

"Happy birt—"

Her sentence was cut short when we heard footsteps in the grass coming our way. We turned around quickly, but only to be shocked at who it was.

Ain't no fuckin' way, I thought as I pulled my Glock from my waist.

To be continued

Up Next!

UP NEXT!

Acknowledgments

Now was that a fire read or what? I'm enjoying the process of writing this series. I hope you all are enjoying reading it. Thank you for turning these pages once again.

I appreciate you all. Without you, there's no P.

-P. Wise

About the Author

Kristen Marin, also known by her pen name P. Wise (Pretti Wise), is an acclaimed author who has achieved national and international success in the arena of fiction writing. Her rich storytelling is a tapestry woven from both her vivid imagination and the diverse experiences she's encountered.

Born in Trinidad and Tobago, Kristen's upbringing in the bustling neighborhood of Bed-Stuy, Brooklyn, and her significant time spent in Philadelphia and Chester have all provided her with a unique lens through which she crafts relatable narratives.

She has always harbored a passion for writing, a love affair that began in her youth with essay writing and maintaining a journal. Kristen's background is rooted in humble beginnings; she stands out as the first in her family not only to earn a college degree but also to endure and overcome the challenges of a federal prison sentence.

Her relentless drive, intelligence, and unwavering determination have carved out her spot in the world of fiction literature, endearing her stories to a wide swath of readers who appreciate her multifaceted viewpoints.

P. Wise has a 3 year old daughter, who's her world and reason for her grind and will to write.

Stay Connected!

Website/Mailing List: PrettiWise.com
Instagram: @CEO.Pwise / @Authoress.P.Wise

STAY CONNECTED!

Facebook: <u>Author P. Wise</u>

Facebook Group: <u>Words of the Wise (P. Wise Book Group)</u>

Email: <u>Author.P.Wise@gmail.com</u>

P.O Box 923
Brookhaven, PA 19015

Also by P. Wise

A Thug Made For Me: A BBW Love Story

Summer Nights between Thick Thighs: A Short BBW Erotica

Pretti & The Beast: An Arranged Marriage

Bound to a Savage

Wet Dreams on Lockdown: Lieutenant Grace (Prequel to Bound to a Savage)

Entangled with a Trinidadian Boss

Melted the Heart of a Menace

My Curves Captivated a Hood Millionaire: A BBW Love Story

My Curves Captivated a Hood Millionaire: A BBW Love Story 2

Come Play In It: An Urban Erotica

Heir to the Plug's Throne

Heir to the Plug's Throne 2

Gorgeous Gangstas

Gorgeous Gangstas 2

Gorgeous Gangstas 3

Luchiano Mob Ties: Snatched Up by a Don Spin-Off

Snatched Up by a Don: A BBW Love Story

Snatched Up by a Don: A BBW Love Story 2

Snatched Up by a Don: A BBW Love Story 3

A Saint Luv'n A Savage: A Philly Love Story

Luv'n a Philly Boss: A Saint Luv'n a Savage Spin-off

Kwon: Clone of a Savage

Kwon: Clone of a Savage 2

Summer Luvin' with a NY Baller

Diary of a Brooklyn Girl

Sex, Scams, & Brisks

Sex, Scams, & Brisks 2